BASIL COPPER

---◆---

IMPACT

Complete and Unabridged

LINFORD
Leicester

First published in Great Britain

First Linford Edition
published 1997

Copyright © 1975 by Basil Copper

British Library CIP Data

Copper, Basil, *1924 –*
Impact.—Large print ed.—
Linford mystery library
1. Detective and mystery stories
2. Large type books
I. Title
823.9′14 [F]

ISBN 0–7089–5070–1

Published by
F. A. Thorpe (Publishing) Ltd.
Anstey, Leicestershire
Set by Words & Graphics Ltd.
Anstey, Leicestershire
Printed and bound in Great Britain by
T. J. International Ltd., Padstow, Cornwall

This book is printed on acid-free paper

1

I GOT in the lobby of the Kuntzler Building and shook the droplets of rain off my trench-coat. Then I rode up in a creaking elevator fifteen floors to the Maroc Trading Company's premises. The operator, who wore a uniform that looked like a reject from Barnum and Bailey's tenting days was a taciturn individual and the other passengers in the elevator were depressed by the weather too, so it wasn't a cheerful ride.

I got out with two old ladies who looked like fugitives from a Marcel Pagnol film and pussy-footed my way down a grey-carpeted corridor which had a glass wall on one side which gave me a good view of L.A. through the rain and the smog. Typewriters were pecking behind closed doors and the corridor was full of secretaries who wore scraped-back hair and were in their fifties. It was that kind of place.

I took off my raincoat and put it over my arm before going up a small staircase at right-angles to the corridor. This passage had no windows and low-wattage bulbs burned in the overhead fittings. The Maroc Trading Company did business behind two cedar-wood doors at the end of the passage. One had Private painted on it in gold curlicue script and the other Reception. I went in the first door and found myself in a big square room with a railed-off enclosure.

There were half a dozen girls sitting pecking at machines in back of the railing and another good view of the smog from the big windows punched in the far wall. The floors were of teak in here and there were some green hot-house plants writhing across the cream walls. Apart from the usual filing cabinets, there were cardboard boxes piled up to the ceiling on my

2

side of the railing and a smell like expensive perfume in the air.

The typing had stopped when I came in. I fought my way past the boxes up to the rail where a tall, well-chiselled blonde wearing a tight black frock stretched over first-rate breasts, had gotten up from her seat and was waiting for me.

"My name's Faraday," I said.

"That must be nice for you," the tall job said pleasantly.

One of the girls behind the rail smiled. She had beautiful teeth. The others went on half-heartedly typing, their ears tuned in my direction.

"Eve Arden did it so much better," I said. "Why not leave it to her?"

The blonde job didn't seem put out. She looked at me approvingly. She had classical features and cobalt-blue eyes that seemed to read the thoughts that were dancing behind my forehead. The dirtier ones anyway.

"You have an appointment, Mr Faraday?"

"Not exactly," I said. "I'm looking for a Mr Albert Troon. He phoned my office this morning."

I got out my wallet and gave the girl one of my business cards, the kind with the classical script and the deckle edges. The blonde job raised her eyebrows. She put out a well-manicured hand and smoothed the material over her taut hips.

"Faraday Investigations?" she said in a mock-conspiratorial voice. "Just what has Mr Troon been doing?"

"That's what I'm here to find out," I said.

The blonde job smiled. She had beautiful teeth too and lips that reminded me of wild berries. Whether they were edible I'd have to find out. I couldn't tell if they were poisonous or not at such short notice.

"My name's Myriam Van Cleef," she said. "I'm supposed to be Mr Troon's Girl Friday. I don't know anything about this. If you'll take a seat for a minute or two I'll go find out."

She waved a hand toward a leather-padded bench against the wall opposite. I thanked her and eased my way over. The tall job went through a door in back. She had a beautiful twelve-cylinder motion. I admired it until the closing door cut the entertainment off. The other girls looked at me for a moment or two and then went on with their typing. I sighed. This was one hell of a way to start a Monday morning.

* * *

I lit a cigarette and put the spent match-stalk back in the box. There was a Pirelli calendar on the wall in rear of the bench. The colour was superb but the angle was making my neck ache so I got up after a bit to have a closer look. I was pretending to examine a water colour of New England in the fall but I wasn't kidding the typists any. When I'd worked out what the girl wearing nothing but rubber boots and a gardening fork was doing, I wandered back along the railing.

Some of the cardboard boxes were open. A giraffe's head was thrust out of one. The eyes looked cold and glazed. There was an elephant's trunk writhing from another. In back of the railing a fox licked his lips, showing a wicked line in teeth. I examined the label on the nearest box. It had printed on it: Maroc Trading Company: Two gross mice. I frowned and went back to my seat. It was one way of making a living I guess.

There was a clicking of heels and the Van Cleef number was wheeling back across the teak floor. She looked a little flushed and the light of battle was in her eye.

"Mr Troon cocked it up again," she told the filing cabinet. She held open the wicket gate in the railing for me.

"Go right on in, Mr Faraday. Mr Troon made the appointment without telling me, of course."

"Of course," I said.

I went through the railing and she closed and latched the wicket behind me.

"Mr Troon difficult?" I said.

The tall blonde clicked her teeth. It was an expressive noise and two of the girls opposite exchanged amused glances.

"It's not so much that he's difficult," she said. "Absent-minded. He'd forget to come to the office if we didn't ring him up and tell him. Even then we don't always win."

"That could be convenient, Miss Van Cleef," I said.

The girl looked me squarely in the eye and winked. It was a nice wink and I warmed to her personality.

"Wait till you meet him, Mr Faraday," she said. "He might just forget to pay your bill."

"That would be a different matter," I said.

We were at the door by this time and the tall job rapped on it. Without waiting she threw it open and marched in. I had a job to keep up with her. The office we were in was a large bright box with white-painted walls. There were cases all around the walls and model soldiers, rubber ducks, every type of mechanical and soft toy, ranged in long lines in the glass cases. Other animals were dumped in writhing masses along the tops of the shelves and even piled over the desk. There was a clucking noise and a small penguin waddled across the carpet and stopped at my feet.

"Fantastic, isn't it?" a voice chuckled.

A man in his shirt-sleeves got up from the carpet and brushed the knees of his trousers.

"We don't know whether we keep the toys for the customers or for him," the Van Cleef girl said drily. She turned up her eyes toward the ceiling.

"Friction-driven, beautifully made, runs for three minutes without stopping and never wears out," the man in shirt-sleeves said enthusiastically. He turned blue, myopic-looking eyes toward me.

They seemed enormous behind the thick-framed lenses he was wearing.

"Does it eat fish?" I said.

The man in shirt-sleeves chuckled.

"Alas, no," he said. "We haven't got around to that yet."

He picked up the penguin with a quick, defensive movement and carried it back over to his desk. He was of medium height and rangily built. He had thin sandy hair that clustered over his skull like moss, indeterminate features and a thin smear of mustache under his nose. He wore a green bow-tie that looked as bright and metallic as some of his own toys.

He cleared a corner of his cluttered desk with a brusque movement of his hand and shrugged into his jacket. He turned around and slumped into his swivel chair.

"I don't remember sending for you, Miss . . . ?" he said mildly.

"Van Cleef," the girl reminded him. "That's your trouble, Mr Troon. You don't remember anything except these wretched toys. This is Mr Faraday."

Troon came forward again and shook hands enthusiastically.

"This is very nice," he said, blinking behind the spectacles. "Friend of Miss Van Cleef's are you? Delightful girl."

The Van Cleef girl looked at both of us pityingly

"You sent for Mr Faraday," she said wearily. "You asked him here."

She looked at me like we were conspirators.

"You'd better sit down, Mr Faraday," she said. "This may take some time."

She took the sandy-haired man by the elbow and propelled him over toward his own desk like he was a child who'd been caught playing with toys that weren't his own.

"Mr Faraday's a private detective, Mr Troon. You must have had some reason for calling him."

Troon's face cleared. He grinned suddenly, and shook his head so hard I figured his spectacles were going to fall off. He frowned out at the rain misting the windows of his office. Beyond the rain was the smog anyway so he wasn't missing much.

"Ah, yes, Mr Faraday, I'm sure I have a note about your visit somewhere. In the meantime Miss Van Cleef will rustle us up some coffee, I'm sure."

He turned back to me.

"You could use a cup?"

"Try me," I said.

Miss Van Cleef looked at me helplessly, shook her head, and went on out. Troon waited until the door had closed behind her. He looked at me for a long moment. The vagueness had gone out of his eyes. They were sharp and piercing behind the glasses. I was surprised at their intensity. Troon sat bolt upright in his seat and folded his hands.

"Now Miss Van Cleef's busy for a moment we can drop all this absent-minded crap, Mr Faraday, and get down to business."

2

"SO you're not really absent-minded?" I said.

Troon chuckled. He sat forward easily, glancing from me to the door and then back again.

"About some things," he said. "I go along with it. It helps."

"Like what for instance?" I said.

Troon leaned over and lowered his voice.

"People get careless when they think the boss is minus a few marbles," he said. "You learn who you can trust. Miss Van Cleef, for instance. She's the tops."

He glanced over at the door again as though he were afraid the tall blonde job might overhear us.

"I had to discharge one girl a month ago for dishonesty."

I leaned back in my leather chair and

reached for my pack.

"Mind if I smoke?"

Troon shook his head. I feathered out blue clouds at the ceiling and put the spent match-stalk in a shallow glass tray perched precariously at the edge of his desk.

"How did you manage that without giving yourself away?" I said.

Troon chuckled again. He examined his immaculate finger-nails as if he expected to find them encrusted with dirt. He flicked an imaginary speck of fluff off his thumb nail and looked at me searchingly.

"I just direct Miss Van Cleef's attention to that area," he said. "She does the rest."

"Smart stuff," I said. "But you still got problems, I take it."

Troon nodded.

"I got problems," he said heavily. "Which is why I asked you over."

"You sure you got the right shop?" I said. "I never had call to investigate a toy factory before. Maybe the teddy bear did it. Whatever it was."

Troon rummaged around in his desk drawer for a minute. He grunted as he came up with a sheet of paper. He put it flat on his blotter and consulted it in silence.

"It's a little more serious than that, Mr Faraday. And I think it will interest you."

"It will interest me, Mr Troon," I said. "Just so long as you don't forget to pay me."

Troon grinned again.

"I don't take my little masquerade that far. I am a bit absent-minded to tell the truth. But not about the things that matter."

He broke off as the door opened again. One of the girls from the outer office came in wheeling a trolley. Troon blinked at her.

"I don't remember asking for you, Miss . . . "

The girl looked conspiratorially at me.

"It's the coffee, Mr Troon. You

ordered it not ten minutes ago."

"Great!" said Troon, rubbing his hands. "Why didn't you say so?"

"You didn't give me a chance, Mr Troon," the girl said calmly. She wheeled the trolley over alongside Troon's desk and busied herself putting out cups and saucers. I noticed there were three lots. She bent down and plugged the coffee percolator into a socket set into the foot of Troon's desk.

"That's just fine," Troon said, rubbing his hands. "I'll ring if I want anything else."

The girl gave me a friendly nod and went clopping out over the teak floor. She passed the Van Cleef girl coming in.

"I wonder you haven't got a clockwork trolley by now," I said.

Troon chuckled.

"We're working on it, Mr Faraday."

He glanced up at the Van Cleef girl as she went over and picked up a cup which he'd just filled. She carried it over to me and put it down on a small stand clamped to the edge of my chair.

"With a doll to pour out?" the Van Cleef number said to me.

"We got the doll, Miss Van Cleef," Troon said, looking at her sharply from under his glasses.

"Why, Mr Troon, I didn't even know you noticed my existence," the tall blonde said. I seemed to detect a faint shade of pink flooding into her cheeks. It looked quite becoming. She turned back to me. Troon seemed to have penetrated her bland façade.

"Cream, sugar, lemon, Mr Faraday?"

"Just a little cream," I said.

I waited while the girl poured from the small silver jug. I looked at Troon with greater respect. He seemed to have a very nice set-up here. Not the sort of business where he was likely to need the services of a private eye. The girl went back to the desk and took the cup her employer handed her.

She took it over to another padded

chair which was at the point of a triangle formed by herself, Troon's desk and my chair. We all sat in that odd way people do when they're gathered in a business office and asked to have coffee with complete strangers. The coffee was good. Troon waved his hand and I went over to the desk and collected my own biscuits. I took the ornamental dish over to the Van Cleef girl. She motioned it away.

"Got to watch my figure."

"I can do that," Troon volunteered gallantly.

The Van Cleef girl made a little clicking noise into her cup.

"It wouldn't do any good, Mr Troon," she said.

She drained her cup and shook her head at Troon's hand proffering the jug. She slid off her chair and on to her feet in one swift, sinuous movement.

"I'd better get on," she said. "Lot to do this morning."

She gave me a frank look across

17

the room. There was genuine liking in her eyes.

"If you want me for note-taking or anything, just buzz."

"I'll do that," Troon said mildly.

He waited until the girl had softly closed the door behind her and then poured me another cup.

"Really nice kid," he said. "And frighteningly efficient." He sighed. "I don't know what I'd do without her."

"Maybe you won't have to," I said.

Troon shot me a look from above his glasses which was razor-sharp.

"Meaning what?"

"Meaning whatever you want it to mean," I said. "I think she's genuinely fond of you."

Troon smiled slowly.

"We'll see," he said. "In the meantime I've got problems. We'd better get down to business."

"That's what I'm here for," I said.

★ ★ ★

18

Troon drummed with thin fingers on the desk before him and consulted the sheet of paper he'd been fooling with before Myriam Van Cleef came in.

"You'll probably think I'm screwy, Mr Faraday, with what I'm going to tell you."

"You let me be the judge of that," I said.

Troon clicked his teeth and focused up his eyes behind the big glasses as he concentrated on the document. He took up a gold-plated pen from a tray on his desk and started scratching out some details on a pad in front of him.

"I'm going to jot down some information for you," he said. "Then you'll know what I'm talking about. Our factory is on the other side of town. I'll give you the address and the manager's name. I'll also write a letter for Maltz which will give you the entree to mooch around there as you want."

He scribbled away for another minute

or two while I looked out at the rain and the smog through the big windows and wondered for the thousandth time why I hadn't taken up some other profession. Troon stopped his scribbling and turned toward me.

"I didn't get your rates, Mr Faraday."

"I didn't give them," I said.

I told him what they were.

"Extra-special services come on top of that," I said. "Those are daily. You want to retain me by the week or the month it comes cheaper."

Troon wrinkled up his brow.

"That's just fine, Mr Faraday. We shan't quarrel over that." He smiled thinly.

"Besides, it comes off tax."

"Everything comes off tax," I said.

Troon turned back to his scribbling.

"You'll want my former partner's name and address," he said. "I'll put that down as well."

"If you wouldn't mind starting at the beginning . . . " I said.

Troon looked at me apologetically.

He took off his heavy glasses and wiped them on a blue-tinted handkerchief he took from his hip pocket.

"I'm sorry, Mr Faraday," he said. "Like I said, you'll probably think the whole thing's nonsense."

He put his glasses back on his nose and folded his hands together on the blotter in front of him.

"The fact is things have been going missing from the factory over the past six months. Whole cases of material, amounting to dozens of gross of articles."

"Like what?" I said.

Troon winced.

"Like three hundred plastic Donald Ducks," he said.

I felt like reaching for my hat right then. But I didn't have a hat so I stayed put.

"Value?"

Troon spread his hands apologetically.

"Practically nothing wholesale. And even less for us to produce. It's just I don't like my wares going astray without my sayso."

"What about the employees?" I said.

"There are about a hundred in the workforce," Troon said. "We have the usual gate security. I can't imagine anybody taking stuff like this out in a van. It would be too risky. Besides, who's going to sell stuff like this? A dollar at a time? It would take years to get rich at that rate."

He shook his head.

"It's more likely to be something less obvious. Apart from the Donalds, there's been toy soldiers and other stuff. Maltz is all right. He's worked for me nearly twenty years. But somebody at managerial level must be involved. Maltz first reported the matter to me."

"And the stuff's still going?" I said.

Troon nodded. "Wholesale. 'Course, somebody might be shipping stuff out by simply altering invoices. It's been done before. But what's the point?"

There was a long silence between us. I was getting the message. I studied the stuff which Troon pushed over toward me. The letter was on one of the official letterheadings of the Maroc Trading Company.

"You said something just now about your former partner," I said.

Troon shrugged. He was silent again for so long that I thought he'd forgotten my question.

"He's a man called Conrad Weinstock," he said. "I'm naturally reluctant to start throwing suspicion about. But I thought the circumstances were relevant."

"I'm listening," I said.

Troon put his hand out to the coffee things on the desk.

"Hit you again?" he said.

"Try me," I said.

I went over to the desk and waited while Troon refilled my cup. I took it and went to gaze out at the rain which was starring the big windows.

"I've given you the details about Weinstock," Troon said. "We never really did hit it off. About six months ago things came to a head."

I took my coffee cup and went back to my chair.

"Care to be more specific?" I said.

Troon put a lean hand up and adjusted his glasses. He glanced over at the toy soldiers on top of the cupboard like he'd rather get back to them than discuss his troubles with me. Their painted features stared soullessly back at us.

"Just a matter of general policy," he said. "Weinstock wanted the firm to go a way I wasn't interested in. Cheap methods and rather trashy toys made of poor materials. I want to expand and make better, more ingenious things. In the end I bought him out."

"What makes you think he'd try to harm the company now?" I said.

Troon lifted his head from his coffee cup and stared at me through his big glasses.

"No reason, really. I've been trying to think of one. But nothing makes sense."

"What's he doing now?" I said.

Troon stirred in his chair.

"He's started another company, I believe."

"In the same field?" I said.

Troon nodded but didn't amplify.

"You think he might be stealing your ideas?"

The lean man chuckled.

"Hardly, Mr Faraday. Hell, anyone could buy my stuff over the counter of any decent toy-store. Besides, we're fully protected by patent. If Weinstock wanted to get in early on new models surely he'd steal one toy which we wouldn't notice, rather than crates-full. I'm not really saying anything against Conrad but I figured I ought to give you the whole picture."

"You did right, Mr Troon," I said. "I won't take up any more of your time."

Troon got up too and shook hands.

"You'll take the case, then?"

"I'll give it a whirl," I said.

3

MYRIAM VAN CLEEF'S well-bred face was a blank mask as she held the door ajar for me as I came out of Troon's office but her eyes were full of curiosity. She was too experienced to ask me anything direct but I could sense the unanswered questions floating above the heads of the other girls as she closed the door behind me.

"Can you spare a minute, Mr Faraday?" she said.

"Sure," I said.

She hesitated and passed a pink tongue across her lips.

"Perhaps you'd better come into my office."

She gestured a well-manicured hand across to an oak door on the other side of the railed-off enclosure. There were so many cardboard cartons of golliwogs

26

piled around it that I'd overlooked it when I came in. The typing went on steadily but I could feel the other girls' eyes boring into my back as I followed the Van Cleef number into the other room. She closed the door behind me and ushered me into a leather chair.

"I have more fun outside with the other girls," she explained. "Trouble is it's too private in here."

She went over and sank into an uncomfortable-looking steel chair on her own side of the desk. It was a small but comfortable office with cream-painted walls and the same rain and smog view of L.A. as Troon's. There were two grey steel filing cabinets; a mahogany desk; two or three leather chairs. Apart from a bowl of roses on the desk and one or two tasteful-looking prints in natural wood frames most of the remaining space was taken up by cartons of toys. They seemed to be everywhere in the Maroc Trading Company's premises. The girl saw my look and grinned again.

"Mr Troon does all his demonstrating around the office," she volunteered. "This is where the buyers come. Mr Troon doesn't like the factory much. He hardly ever goes there."

"Sensible man," I said. "Especially with the talent available in the office."

The Van Cleef girl smiled again, more distantly this time.

"I expect you wondered why I asked you in here," she began.

"I can guess," I said. "You're a little curious perhaps and knowing Mr Troon's absent-mindness."

The tall girl shook her head.

"Not entirely that, Mr Faraday," she said. "Mind if I smoke?"

I got out my matches and lit the cigarette she held out to the flame. The rich aroma of Turkish tobacco started to permeate the office. I waved her proffered pack away.

"I'd prefer to smoke my own," I said.

The girl inserted the Turkish cigarette into a long, gold-plated holder and clamped it between her white teeth. She looked more like Eve Arden than ever. She blinked her cobalt-blue eyes at me like she was having trouble focusing her thoughts.

"I wouldn't like it noised around but I'm rather fond of Mr Troon," she said.

"So I gathered," I told her.

Myriam Van Cleef looked startled.

"Does it show?" she said.

"You're just a little bit too emphatic and brisk with him," I said. "I've had long experience of this sort of thing. You know, dolls and characters working together in offices."

The Van Cleef girl grinned.

"Sure," she said. "You look like a regular marriage broker."

I let that one pass.

"So you're very fond of Mr Troon," I said.

The girl nodded.

"It's none of my business why you're here, Mr Faraday. And I'm not asking you to divulge any secrets. Mr Troon will tell me when he's ready, I guess."

"But you'd appreciate a crumb from my table when I'm in a position to tell you anything," I finished for her.

The blonde girl looked relieved. She flicked the ash off her cigarette into a small jar held by a fluffy-looking bear. Even the ashtrays in Troon's place had to be different.

"Something like that," she said. "I have to tie all the ends together around here and I spend more than half my time fussing over Mr Troon."

"Perhaps that's the trouble," I said.

The Van Cleef girl flushed.

"I could take offence at that, Mr Faraday, but I presume you meant it kindly," she said softly.

"Sure," I said, getting up.

"You're trying too hard. Mr Troon's a little myopic as well as absent-minded. He's the sort of man who has to have things thrust forcibly to his attention."

The Van Cleef girl was smiling.

"I see what you mean but it might

be a little difficult in practice. You wouldn't care to give me a lesson one evening?"

"I'm not an expert, Miss Van Cleef," I said. "But for you I'd make an effort any time."

The Van Cleef number got up with a rustling of skirts.

"That's always nice to know," she said.

We were standing close together near the door when there came a timid knocking. The blonde girl opened it a little sharply I thought. One of the girls from the main office was hovering outside.

"It's the factory, Miss Van Cleef," she said. "They won't speak to anyone but you."

The blonde job sighed and looked at me regretfully.

"You see how it is, Mr Faraday. We'll get together again some time."

"Real soon," I said.

I smiled at both ladies and opened the wicket and went on out. I rode down in the elevator with a couple of characters from Rebecca of Sunnybrook Farm. It seemed like the building was inhabited mainly by magazines for the elderly. But perhaps I was wrong. Judging by the personnel at Maroc Trading Company anyway.

It was still raining when I went out. I sighed and splashed my way back to the Buick. Monday is one day which should be taken out the calendar.

* * *

It was early afternoon. I'd gotten outside a steak and a blueberry pie special at an off-stem dinette and I felt I might last through until tea-time. Even the rain was beginning to let up. I was sitting back at my battered broadtop resting my eyes by tracing the cracks in the ceiling and varying this by watching the stalled traffic on the boulevard below. As an occupation it wasn't much but it was all I had for the moment.

Around three the outer office door clicked and Stella came in. She looked clean and bright and shining and little drops of moisture were glinting on the bobbled Scottish-style tam-o-shanter she was wearing. She grinned when she saw me and put down her shopping basket on her own desk.

"Monday," she said. "I should have left you with some bills to sign."

"I'm plenty busy," I said. "There's a lot of thought going on inside this skull."

"I'll bet," Stella said darkly.

I took my feet down from the desk. Stella took off the bobbled wool hat and shook it. The gold bell of her hair shone like metal beneath the lamps.

"We got a heavy case," I said.

Stella looked at me doubtfully but she didn't say anything.

"I went down to the Maroc Trading Company's place this morning," I said.

"That must have been nice," Stella said politely.

"It was," I said. "That was just what

the tall number at the desk said."

Stella raised her eyebrows. She went over to hang up her slicker. She was wearing a thin white silk sweater and a dark grey mini-skirt today. She looked so bright that she shot the melancholy of Monday all to shreds.

"You want to tell me about it?"

"Over coffee," I said.

Stella smiled again.

"It's a deal."

She went over and I heard the click as she switched on the percolator in the glassed-in alcove where we do the brewing-up. I looked thoughtfully over at my large-scale map of L.A. while Stella clattered about with the cups. Presently a pleasant aroma began to penetrate the office. Stella came back and sat down at her desk opposite me. She patted an imaginary hair into place on her immaculate head.

"So what does the Maroc Trading Company do with itself?"

"Toys and novelties," I said.

Stella looked at me incredulously.

"That's what I thought," I said. "Someone's been stealing consignments of Donald Ducks from their factory."

"You're joking," Stella said.

Little lights were dancing in back of her eyes.

"I wish I were," I said. "We need the money this time of year."

"That bad?" Stella said.

"The company's run by a man named Troon," I said. "He thinks his ex-partner might be behind it."

Stella got up again and went back behind the alcove. She fooled around with cups and saucers. She came back and put the steaming cup on my blotter, went over to get her own. When she'd settled again she looked at me thoughtfully.

"The Brothers Grimm might be behind it, Mike," she said. She shook her head. "Donald Duck hi-jackers. That's a new low, even for us."

"The whole thing's screwy," I said. "Even Troon admitted that. But it might be interesting."

"We must need the work badly," Stella said.

She went on stirring her coffee with a long-handled spoon and pushed over the box of biscuits toward me. I got up and took them from her desk. I went back and sat down and took the first sip of coffee. Like always it was pretty good.

"We do," I said, answering her question.

I got out the stuff Troon had written for me and flipped it over to Stella. She raked the sheets toward her and studied them thoughtfully while she sipped.

"Make a note of those when you get a minute and give me the relevant material back," I said.

Stella reached for her pad and scribbled. I got through my coffee and looked over toward the window where the rain was still spatting the panes. My mind was a blank today like the weather. Ten minutes must have gone by in dead silence while Stella scribbled on. She looked up suddenly.

"Like another?"

I nodded. She took my cup and clopped over to the alcove.

"So what's your first call, Conrad Weinstock or the factory?" she said.

"I feel like taking in a movie," I said.

Stella re-appeared and put the full cup down on my blotter. She grinned.

"Who doesn't on a wet Monday?" she said. "But that won't pay the rent."

"You win," I said. "Which is the nearest?"

Stella smiled again.

"I looked it up. Weinstock. The factory's way on the other side of town."

I lifted my cup, looking at the rain-smeared windows again.

"Weinstock it is," I said.

4

CONRAD WEINSTOCK lived at Apartment 42 in the Bixby Apartments, a chintzy lay-out off one of the main stems. The rain had stopped and the pavements were already dry when I slotted the Buick into a vacant space and got out. The Apartments had chromed-steel canopies over the windows and a red and white striped awning from the entrance across the sidewalk down to the taxi-rank. I strolled on over, avoiding the puddles and admiring the tone of the whole place.

The name of the Apartments was scribed in heavy gold-tinted script across the front of the massive chrome portico. Steel-framed swing doors led to the interior. A Vice-Admiral swathed in braid to his elbows wasn't exactly killing himself to usher me into the vestibule.

I guessed he figured I wasn't worth it. He figured right. I went on in without his help and fought my way across the heavy pile carpet toward the reception desk.

There were white leather divans dotted about the vestibule and several wax dummies sitting around giving very good imitations of old gentlemen reading newspapers. There were a couple of middle-aged matrons with anxious expressions standing near the desk. Both had white poodles on leashes and were discussing the prospects of a promenade without getting the animals drowned. I waited until they'd settled this important question and then tackled the clerk.

He was a small, rabbit-faced man with protruding teeth and a mass of dark, heavily pomaded hair. The top of his head was so highly polished it reflected back the lighting in a series of dazzling pin-points. I'd bet he spent hours buffing it before he came on duty. He gave me a grade-two smile like he figured I was a non-profit making customer. He was right at that.

"I'm looking for a Mr Weinstock," I said.

The clerk snittered to himself like I'd said something funny. He ruffled a sheet of papers on the counter in front of him and crinkled up his face like he was having to solve abstruse equations. It didn't make him look any prettier.

"Now, Mr Weinstock," he said in a high, squeaky voice. "Let me see . . . "

"How many you got?" I said. "Mr Conrad Weinstock. He lives in Apartment Forty-two."

The clerk's rabbit teeth dug viciously into his lower lip.

"Oh, that Mr Weinstock," he said like a great truth had just struck him.

I was having difficulty in restraining myself from striking him too.

"It's Monday, sonny," I said. "It's been a lousy day so far. Don't make it any worse."

I must have put on my Humphrey

Bogart expression or something because the clerk gave me a bolt-eyed look. I was getting tired of his expressions.

"If you'll forgive me, sir," he said with dignity. "I was thinking of Mr Horace Weinstock, one of our long-term residents. Mr Conrad Weinstock only moved in about six months ago."

"Your apology accepted," I said. "Is he in or out?"

The clerk threw out his chest like a pouter-pigeon.

"If you'll wait a moment I'll go find out," he said. "Whom shall I say?"

"Don't bother to announce me," I said. "I just want to know if he's home."

I slid my hand across the counter and tickled the back of the clerk's hand with the edge of the green-back. It had an electric effect on him. He glanced down and a beatific expression spread over his features. The bill seemed to melt beneath his finger tips so fast I didn't even see it go.

"Why didn't you say so before, sir," he said with an oily smile.

"Mr Weinstock came in half an hour ago. Fourth floor, fourth door on the right. Take the elevator opposite."

"All it takes is money," I said.

"Money's at the back of everything," the clerk said.

His snigger followed me over to the elevator. I hung around just long enough to see he didn't use the telephone. When I was sure he wasn't announcing my arrival I got in the nearest cage and buttoned my way up to the fourth floor. I got out the mahogany and rosewood box and found myself in a marble-floored corridor. Diffused lighting came from concealed fittings overhead and the corridor itself was lined with what looked like genuine oil paintings.

Moderns, of course. Even the Bixby Apartments wouldn't leave old masters lying around. I figured these were by artists who hadn't made it yet. I looked at a blank canvas in a metal anodised frame for several minutes. It was signed Van Houten in the bottom righthand corner.

I heard footsteps scuffing on the marble behind me. I turned around. A plump man with a red face, dressed in a mustard yellow suit squinted past me at the picture.

"Jesus Christ," he said softly. "What they get up to nowadays. The guy who made the frame had more talent. They're conmen, not artists."

"I take it you wouldn't bid for it?" I said.

The fat man turned even pinker.

"Take my advice, young man and keep your savings in steel and gilt-edged," he snapped. "Then you'll be able to afford to live at the Bixby Apartments when you're retired."

He stumped off down the corridor and thumbed the elevator button.

"Though it's not so hot here, come to think of it," the pink man said as a parting gift.

I grinned. I watched him stump into

the elevator. He whined downwards out of sight. I went back along the corridor and found Apartment 42. I thumbed the satinsteel bellpush and waited for someone to show. I didn't have to wait long. The door was opened almost immediately by a tall, dark-haired man with a thick black mustache. He was about fifty and had a wary look on his face and a durable air about him that put me on my guard.

"Mr Weinstock?" I said.

The big man fiddled with the edge of the door like I'd said something libellous. He nodded, frowning.

"Yes," he said in a low voice. "What do you want?"

"Nothing that will cost you anything, Mr Weinstock," I said. "Just a few minutes of your time."

Weinstock nodded again. The lamplight from the room beyond shone on his slicked-back hair. It reminded me of the desk clerk down below. He cleared his throat.

"I'm listening," he said.

44

"I don't propose to talk out here," I said.

The big man looked at me sharply. He seemed to take me in for the first time.

His eyes narrowed and he cleared his throat.

"What's it about?" he said warily.

"Tell you just as soon as we get inside," I said.

He hesitated so long I almost went to sleep. Then he stepped back awkwardly.

"You'd better come on in."

"I was hinting that way for the past couple of minutes," I said.

Weinstock scowled. It didn't make him look any more attractive.

"Don't get fresh with me, mister," he said nastily. "You'll find it won't pay."

"You're frightening me," I said.

The big man flushed and I saw his fists ball in the pockets of the dark blue dressing gown he was wearing over his cream shirt and red tie. He bit back what he was going to say and slammed the door behind me. It was a pretty plushy lay-out.

The room was about forty feet square and white-painted wrought iron balustrades writhed their way down into the living area from the platform on which we were standing. There was a white marble fireplace, a few good oils on the walls and lots of white rugs and cushions lying about. I followed Weinstock down the staircase to where a colour television set was blaring trivialities into the early evening air.

Weinstock flipped a switch on the end of a long cable and silence flooded in. He didn't say anything so I stood and admired the view of the city from the big picture windows at the side of the room. There was a green leather divan about half a mile long in the centre of the room and Weinstock went and sat down on it, thrusting out his heels on to the white rug in front of him like he was having trouble holding on to his temper.

There were drapes up at the far end of the room which was in shadow and other doors led off. I looked at myself in a gilt antique mirror; I looked hard-faced and sardonic like usual. I sighed and went over and planted my size nines in front of Weinstock. It was then I noticed a pair of girl's panties lying on the divan next the big man. They were jazzily striped and they were lying like they'd been hurriedly stripped off.

I grinned. I realised now why Weinstock was so badtempered. I just had time to notice the empty bottle and the two half-full glasses on the table before the big man got it. He reached out almost casually and scooped up the panties. He slid them into his dressing-gown pocket like they were a handkerchief which he'd laid down there a moment ago. He picked up his glass and frowned into it as he drank.

"I'd offer you one but you look like you don't drink so early in the day," he said.

"That's right," I told him. "Mustn't spoil the clean-cut look. It's bad for the customers."

Weinstock put his glass down on the table in front of him and looked at me steadily.

"Meaning what?"

"Meaning I'd like you to answer a few questions," I said.

Weinstock shook his head. Red was starting to suffuse the skin of his neck.

"Supposing I don't want to answer?"

"Nobody's forcing you," I said.

Weinstock sneered.

"Too right," he sneered. "You a cop or something?"

"Private," I said.

Weinstock sneered again. His expressions were getting monotonous.

"I could take you and bounce you out on your ear," he said.

"You could try," I said evenly.

We traded glances for a minute or so; he was the first to drop his eyes.

"You haven't heard me yet," I said.

"It might be good news."

"It never is," Weinstock said sullenly. "I'm listening."

"You used to be partners with a man named Albert Troon in a toy factory," I said.

Weinstock stared at me with smouldering eyes.

"Not that again," he said.

"I didn't know you'd had any trouble," I said.

Weinstock looked at me evenly.

"No trouble," he said. "Nothing that I can't handle."

He held out one thick-fingered hand toward me.

"Before we start anything I want to know who I'm talking to."

"Sure," I said. "That's fair enough."

I got out the photostat of my licence in the perspex holder and passed it over to him. He sat studying it for a minute or two, saying nothing. There were two small patches of dull red on his cheekbones now. They might have been caused by alcohol. On the other

49

hand it might have been something else. He passed back the folder to me and lifted his glass to his mouth.

"So Albert's at it again," he said. "Always suspicious, always worried someone going to do him down."

"You've had trouble?" I said.

"Nothing really," Weinstock said.

He looked at me for a long moment; the corners of his mouth crinkled up in a minuscule smile.

"Though why the hell I'm telling you all this I don't know."

"You're impressed with my clean-cut looks," I suggested.

Weinstock shrugged. His smile grew.

"Something like that," he said.

He lifted the glass again.

"You want some? Help yourself. There's a decanter over there."

"Not this time of the afternoon," I said. "I reserve it for after office hours."

"Suit yourself," Weinstock said.

"You started another toy firm, I believe," I said.

"It's no secret," Weinstock said. "It's all on the record."

He stopped suddenly and put his glass down with a sudden rap on the table.

"Has Troon got some idea I'm trying to copy some of his patents? Because if so . . ."

"It's nothing like that, Mr Weinstock," I said. "He just called me in on a routine check. As part of that check I'm seeing people who worked for or had some connection with Mr Troon. You were his partner. You come within that category."

"Sounds reasonable," Weinstock said. "But you'd better spit it out. I haven't got all night."

"Some shipments of toys have been going astray from the factory," I said. "I just wondered if you had any ideas."

Weinstock looked at me with hard eyes.

"This Troon's idea or yours?" he said.

"Mine," I said. "You know a great

deal about the factory, obviously. As a partner you'd be up to all the wrinkles employed by staff who wanted to cheat on the owners. I'd be obliged for your help."

Weinstock held my eyes with his own. He was smiling now.

"You're a crafty bastard, Faraday," he said. "You like to get the suspect on your side, don't you?"

I walked over and sat down on the other arm of the settee, facing him.

"It's not a question of suspicion, Mr Weinstock. Is it likely a partner would be interested in a few cartons of cheap toys? What I'd like to know is your ideas on the subject."

Weinstock got up and stood looking down at me. He rubbed his strong chin with a heavy hand. A door closed softly in the apartment somewhere.

"I shan't keep the lady waiting long," I said.

Weinstock grinned again.

"Pretty good at your job are you, Faraday?"

"Not bad," I said. "I manage to scrape along."

Weinstock sat down. He crossed one leg over the other and sat frowning at the white rug in front of him.

"Pushers sometimes use plastic toys to stow drugs in for shipment," he said. "Not through Customs or across borders, of course. But just for convenience' sake, in case anyone calls."

"I know that," I said.

"I figured you would," Weinstock said.

He leaned back on the divan and frowned again.

"There's one big snag about this story," he said. "Any pusher who's not bombed out of his mind would make sure he bought the toys for the job. He wouldn't steal them."

"I figured that too," I said.

Weinstock looked at me quizzically. He glanced from me toward the shadowy door of the room opposite and then back again.

"We got quite a problem," he said.

5

WEINSTOCK sat and studied me through a haze of tobacco smoke. He'd mellowed surprisingly in the past hour. He seemed to have forgotten about the girl waiting in the other room. Leastways, if there was a girl in the other room. It could have been my suspicious mind. But few men of my acquaintance use women's underwear as handkerchiefs. Not those outside the funny farm at any rate. It was dark now and red and green neon made vibrating patterns in the dusk outside the window.

They tinged Weinstock's face with bars of colour so that he looked like one of Troon's more macabre toys in the dimly-lit apartment. I had a glass at my elbow now in deference to the hour. I couldn't make Weinstock out for the moment. I decided to reserve judgment. There must be a reason for his sudden amiability.

"What's your new company, Mr Weinstock?" I said.

The big man sat forward and tapped out his ash in the tray on the table in front of him.

"Arco Toys," he said. "I haven't got a partner this time. That way we got no clash of ideas."

"What was the real trouble between you and Troon?"

Weinstock wrinkled up his eyes.

"Like I said earlier, no real trouble. It was just a clash of personalities. Troon wanted to concentrate on complicated and expensive toys. They had a lot of charm, sure. And at the right price and in the right market they'd be great. But they cost too much to produce. And they were taking up too much time ironing out the problems."

Weinstock sat back again and looked at me like we were used to having a friendly business conference on occasion.

"Whereas I go for cheaper stuff, unbreakable, easily made and easily sold. So if you get stuck you don't go down the plug-hole. You take the Christmas trade, for example . . . "

"You take it, Mr Weinstock," I said. "We're getting a little off the point."

"Sure, Mr Faraday," Weinstock said amiably. "Have another drink."

An hour ago he'd have blown his top if I'd stopped him in full-flow like that. But he was on his own topic now. Like most men on their speciality he forgot everything else in his enthusiasm. Weinstock lifted his glass and took a long gulp like all this talking had tired him.

"You wanted some angles about Troon's missing material?"

"If it's no trouble," I said.

"No trouble," Weinstock said.

He got up and stretched himself, his shadow huge on the floor in the light of the shaded lamps. He looked at his watch.

"Excuse me a couple of minutes,

Mr Faraday. I'll be right back."

I watched him amble up the staircase. He carried his drink in his right hand, his left in the pocket of his dressing gown. I figured he was on the level.

Telling him about Troon's troubles didn't matter either way. If he had nothing to do with it he might come up with some ideas. If he had a hand, my nosing in might betray him into a careless move. Either way suited me. I waited until I heard the door close in the distance. Then I got up casually and put my drink down on the table.

I went up the staircase as softly as I could, trying the treads, moving one foot at a time. I stopped on the landing and then went on over toward the door through which Weinstock had just disappeared. I could hear the faint murmur of voices. I was on carpeting now so I got as near to the door as I could without committing myself and pretended to examine a painting in a gilt rococo frame.

One of the voices was Weinstock's,

the other a woman's. The girl sounded petulant.

"You gonna sit there on your ass all night and swap reminiscences with any bum who happens in here?" she said.

Weinstock's voice was placatory.

"I couldn't help it, honey," he said. "There's been some trouble up at Troon's plant. He sent a gumshoe around asking questions. Just a routine thing. I'm giving him a few ideas."

"I'll be giving you a few if you don't get the lead out," the girl squawked. "We were supposed to be having a good screw this afternoon."

I grinned. I went back down the staircase as quickly and quietly as I could. I was still sitting there swilling my drink when Weinstock showed five minutes later. He had a red flush on his cheeks and there was an angry look in his eyes. I made a sympathetic face. Weinstock looked at me for a moment. Then he sat down on the divan again and poured himself another drink.

"The hell with dames," he said.

"Now, where were we?"

"Talking about missing Donald Ducks," I said.

Weinstock grinned.

"Screwiest thing I ever heard," he said. "Tell you one thing, though. Management wouldn't be interested."

"Truck drivers?" I said.

Weinstock nodded.

"Someone could be altering delivery sheets," he said. "It's been done. Though why, I wouldn't know. Somebody must be hard up for a few dollars."

I sat back and frowned at my toe-caps. Weinstock sat and watched me warily over the rim of his glass.

"How about explosives?" I said.

Weinstock blinked.

"I don't quite follow you."

"The profit motive wouldn't come into it, according to you," I said. "That was Troon's view also. Such toys as went missing were all cheap plastic things. So we can rule out the profit motive or petty pilfering, right?"

Weinstock wrinkled up his face like he was having difficulty following my train of thought.

"So we come up with the toys as containers for something," he said.

"Exactly," I told him. "You've already mentioned drug-pushers. What about explosives?"

Weinstock's face cleared.

"You mean Arab terrorists?"

"Anybody," I said. "Airline hi-jackers, for example. They walk on to an aircraft with a child. One of those plastic toys filled with explosives and carried by a child wouldn't arouse any suspicion."

Weinstock's eyes were shrewd and clear now.

"You got a nasty mind, Mr Faraday," he said.

"It's my job," I said.

"We still get back to the method," Weinstock said morosely. "All we got for starters is a few cases of plastic toys going missing. Now we got on to drug containers and airline hi-jackers.

We still get back to the basics. Why the hell risk stealing such stuff when a real crook would buy such toys over the counter."

"He might not," I said. "They'd be more easily traceable that way. Suppose he wanted a lot?"

Weinstock was silent for a long moment. He shifted his feet carefully on the rug in front of the divan and squinted at his glass.

"You sure you don't suspect me?" he said softly.

"I wouldn't put you on your guard if I did," I said. "And I wouldn't come up here alone without a good case. All we're doing is kicking a few ideas around. Besides, you got your own toy set-up now. You wouldn't need any of Troon's stuff."

Weinstock grinned suddenly.

"Right enough," he said. "You got a business card? If I come up with any ideas I'll give you a ring."

I got out one of my cards with the curlicue script and passed it over

61

to him. I finished off my drink. I looked at the neons vibrating out in the dark beyond the window and sighed. I thanked Weinstock and got up and went out. I rode down in the elevator little wiser than when I'd gone in. That was Monday. Tuesday wouldn't be better. I'd got Troon's toy factory to look forward to tomorrow.

* * *

The Maroc Trading Company's layout was a bigger setup than I'd expected. The factory covered about three acres. It was about a two-hour drive south toward Inglewood. I pulled off the main stem following the instructions Troon had given me and drove in the general directions of Hughes Airport. The day was dry but the smog lying over the landscape was blurring the outlines of the distant hills and smuts coming in round the Buick's windshield made the eyes smart.

I pulled off into a layby to consult

Troon's sketch-map and took a breather. The traffic went by on the highway in a muffled roar and far off I could see a big jet beginning its run in to L.A. I lit a cigarette and feathered blue smoke out over my upholstery. I ran over the facts about Troon's case. If you could call it a case. That took about three seconds flat. I looked at Troon's plan again and found the turn I wanted.

I gunned back into the traffic and fought my way toward a series of silver gas-tanks belonging to some chemical plant which dominated the horizon. I could smell the place long before I got there. Troon's factory was about ten miles beyond, on a secondary road in a wilderness of prefabricated buildings and industrial development.

I pulled the Buick in to an asphalt driveway that led to a high, wire-mesh fence. The gates were wide open but there was a white-painted wooden barrier which had painted on it in black letters: *ALL VISITORS HALT*. The legend: Maroc Trading Company was carried on a white circular arch which curved above the entrance gates. All I could see from here was a few low buildings and half a dozen trucks parked in a bay farther down. The faint hum of machinery drifted over.

There was a small wooden shed set next the gate and a big negro in green coveralls shuffled out and eased round the end of the wooden barrier. He was pleasant enough though despite his size and he listened impassively as I told him what I wanted.

"Just hang on mister and I'll let Mr Maltz know you're here," he said.

I switched off the motor and got out and stretched my legs while the big man went back in the shed. I could see him on the phone through the dusty side-window. He came back in about three minutes. I finished my cigarette and ground the butt beneath my heel. The negro screwed up his eyes like the sun was hurting him. His white teeth flashed beneath his short beard.

"Go right in man and follow the

road around to Admin. You can't miss it. You'll see a door marked Reception and they'll tell you how to find Mr Maltz."

I thanked him and got back in the Buick. I started the engine and eased up to the barrier. It must have been worked from inside the shed because it went up of its own accord. I drove through and followed the asphalt drive like the gateman had said. The sun was bright and clear now and it winked back blindingly off the glazed skylights in the low factory buildings and from the white-painted walls.

I eased past the lorry-park and across a loading bay where two scarlet fork-lift trucks were hefting big crates of Troon's toys into the trucks. More Donald Ducks I imagined. I grinned suddenly. I had a mental picture of Troon down on his hands and knees with the mechanical penguin. It seemed one hell of a way to make a living. But no crazier than mine I guessed.

Shaved turf was coming up now

and the drive split into two, circling a complex of grass, flower-beds and administrative buildings. There was even a couple of fountains sparkling in the sunshine, the spray descending in rainbow clouds on to the grass.

I grunted and pulled up the Buick in front of the reception area. My thoughts were scattered. You'll be wandering lonely as a cloud in a minute, Faraday, I told myself. There were a couple of Mercedes and a Rolls parked with the dozen or so cars in the reserved lot in front of Maroc's Headquarters.

I figured the Rolls would belong to Maltz. I upgraded Troon another two notches. If his manager could afford this type of transport Troon must be in a big bracket. Though probably the British car belonged to a visiting Japanese salesman. I pulled my thoughts together and went up the flight of shallow cement steps and into the coolness of the interior.

6

THEY didn't waste time on chintzy lay-outs here. The office had a woodblock floor with a divan and a few potted plants dotted about but there were still the cardboard cartons full of toys. They were scattered thickly against the walls like they were waiting to be collected. There were glass cubicles in back and typewriters going. A dark-haired number with a heavily made-up face was buffing her nails with a sanding board and making heavy weather of it. She hardly paused to change gear on the gum in her mouth as I came up.

"Right on in," she said, jerking her thumb. "Mr Maltz is expecting you."

I walked on over to a plain oak door which had the legend: General Manager Rodney Maltz painted on it in severe black lettering. I knocked and a voice barked "Come."

Maltz's office was about ten by ten and evidently designed for results. There were two steel filing cabinets, a modern teak desk, a couple of chairs and a fine view of chimneys through the unfrosted upper half of his office window. Maltz was a muscular-looking tanned individual with a barrel chest and plenty of hair around his throat.

I know because he had his coat off and no tie and his shirt sleeves rolled up to the elbows to expose his strong, muscular arms. He wore a gold wristlet watch on his left wrist and dark glasses, despite the dimness of the office.

His thinning hair was reddish and cut fairly short. I should have said he was around forty and pretty fit. He looked like a character who worked out regularly. He had strong, open features and square white teeth with a gap in the middle. There were reddish patches over his cheek-bones which could have been caused by sun and wind; or maybe he got them in the ring. He eased up from behind the desk with a curt manner and put out a strong hand for me to shake.

"This is a load of nonsense, Mr Faraday," he said in a low, growling voice. "But I expect you know that yourself."

"I don't know anything yet, Mr Maltz," I said.

I sank into the chair indicated by Maltz. His eyebrows went up in surprise.

"Surely Mr Troon told you why he called you in?"

He put out his hands on the desk in an expressive gesture.

"A few cartons of toys. I ask you."

His breath went out in a whoosh of silent laughter.

"It might be trivial as industrial pilfering goes," I said. "But theft's theft. And if Mr Troon wants me to look around . . . "

Maltz coughed suddenly, like he was embarrassed.

"Sure, Mr Faraday, I take your

point. But it seems so crazy to me. And we got other problems. Like selling against fierce competition."

"And you don't want a private eye nosing around the factory," I said. "Why don't you come out and say so?"

Maltz sat up bolt upright in his chair like he was ready to fly at my throat. I couldn't see the expression in his eyes behind the dark cheaters but his facial muscles weren't indicating pleasure. But all he said in a grumbling voice was, "Don't get me wrong, Mr Faraday."

"I'm trying not to," I said. "I hope you haven't told anyone around the factory that I'm coming."

Maltz looked embarrassed again.

"Only Reynolds, my overseer," he said.

"Thanks," I told him. "Why didn't you put a notice on the front gate while you were at it."

There was a heavy silence. Before Maltz could say anything I started off again.

"Sure, you can't see any point," I

said. "But this is Troon's business and mine. I'm the professional and you're cutting my throat before I start. You might just as well tell the thief I'm coming. I understood from Troon you were discreet."

I was enjoying myself by now and the burning patches on Maltz's cheeks were even pinker. He cleared his throat with a low rasp.

"You got no call to talk like that, Mr Faraday."

"I'll talk any way I like," I said. "We'll see what Troon thinks of the set-up."

I got up. My act was going over great. Maltz suddenly looked alarmed. He got up too. He was a much smaller man than I'd figured.

"Maybe I was wrong, Mr Faraday," he said hastily. "I'm not used to this sort of thing. Perhaps I didn't take it seriously enough."

There were lights glittering somewhere in behind the blank stare of the cheaters.

"You haven't had much experience managing factories," I said.

"What do you mean by that?" Maltz barked.

I really had him stirred up now. His chest was rising and falling beneath his shirt in time with his indignation.

"Pilfering's one of the most common things in a factory," I said.

"Oh, that," Maltz said. He grinned suddenly.

"I usually deal with that myself. I kinda lean on them and then throw them out on their ear."

I grinned too. Maltz looked like a fighting cock as he stood quivering across from me.

"And you think that's what we ought to do in this case," I said. "Let's call a truce, Mr Maltz. Sorry if I got under your skin."

Maltz smiled again. He looked happier now.

"I'm sorry too, Mr Faraday. I didn't mean to queer your pitch."

I sat down and Maltz followed suit.

He slid over a box of cigars from his side of the desk. I shook my head. I got out my own pack as he lit up. There were blue clouds shimmering over our heads before I spoke again.

"This may seem like small stuff to you, Mr Maltz. But there might be something deeper behind it. That's why I didn't want anybody else but you to know."

Maltz nodded. His red hair shone vividly in the light of the sun spilling through the window.

"I shouldn't think there'd be any harm done. Reynolds is pretty tight-mouthed. I wouldn't like this to get back to Mr Troon."

"Maybe it won't have to," I said.

Maltz folded his broad-fingered hands on the desk in front of him and looked at me shrewdly. Leastways, that's what I figured he was doing. I still couldn't see his eyes behind the thick lenses.

"Meaning what, Mr Faraday?"

"Depends on the degree of co-operation," I said.

Maltz leaned back comfortably in his chair.

"I got all the records and confidential files on every employee right here in the office," he said. "Ask away."

★ ★ ★

I sifted through the sheaf of papers on the desk in front of me. My second cup of coffee stood at my elbow. Maltz sat and watched me closely. The butt of his second cigar was clamped between his teeth and the air was close and heavy despite the fans going. I looked at my watch. It was after six now.

"Am I keeping you?" I said.

Maltz shook his head.

"I don't usually leave until around eight anyway. We work shifts here when the pressure is on. The place closes at midnight, except for maintenance and the guards."

I nodded.

"Business that good?"

Maltz puffed on his cigar until a

small shower of sparks shot out over his desk surface.

"Mr Troon is a very clever man," he said. "And some of the mechanical toys are very ingenious. They sell well for such expensive items. But our mass market is with the cheaper stuff."

"That's why Weinstock left?" I said.

Maltz spread out his hands like he was a diplomat at U.N.O.

"It's really not for me to say, Mr Faraday. But you made a good guess."

"I already saw Weinstock," I said. "That's what he said."

Maltz looked at me admiringly.

"You don't waste much time, Mr Faraday," he said.

"That's what I'm paid for," I said.

I turned back to the personal records of the fifteen truck drivers Troon employed.

"This the lot? They don't seem over-many for a business this size."

Maltz took the cigar out of his mouth.

"We're a little under-staffed on that side. We usually reckon to run about twenty drivers, to allow for sickness, holidays and so forth."

"Any leave recently?" I said.

"Two about six months ago," he said. "But we had toys go missing since then, if that's what you're getting at."

I tapped the sheaf of papers in my hand.

"You got one driver here — Curtis. I see he did a short stretch one time for petty larceny."

An expression of slight irritation crossed Maltz's face.

"We already thought of that, Mr Faraday. Curtis got mixed up in some warehouse-breakings, true. But that was years ago. He's had a clean sheet for the past ten years."

"So far as you know," I said. "You didn't question him?"

Maltz shook his head.

"Mr Troon isn't that green, Mr Faraday. We kept an eye on

him. But we didn't come up with anything."

"All right," I said.

I stabbed at Curtis's record sheet. "This is where I start."

7

I TURNED the Buick's bonnet back in the direction of the entrance and crept into a corner of the loading bay. I killed the motor. A thin humming sound from Troon's factory went up into the night sky. Lights sparkled round the perimeter of the wire fence and made pale moons in the deep blue dusk. Despite the industrial background I could smell the perfume of tropical flowers from somewhere in the hills beyond.

I lit a cigarette, shielding the flame carefully with my cupped hands. I glanced at my watch. It was now 8.15 p.m. and the man I wanted would be making for L.A. in fifteen minutes. I'd checked out with Maltz and he'd given me a list of his calls for the evening. I'd decided to follow Curtis on his round. It probably wouldn't lead to anything but I had to start somewhere. If Curtis made good time he'd finish around eleven-thirty. Then he'd start back to the factory and I'd call it a day.

He only had six calls to make and I'd already routed them on a sheet of paper. If Curtis followed the logical geographical sequence he'd hit the locations I'd marked at around the times I'd worked out. If he deviated it might mean something else. Or not. I sighed. It was that kind of an assignment.

Privately, I agreed with Maltz. It did seem pretty trivial. But I had to see it through. That was what Troon was paying me for. I glanced at my watch again. Only four minutes had crawled by. I checked the route I'd pencilled under the shaded dash-light. Curtis was due to make his first drop at around ten. This was several crates of toys at a place called La Boutique Fantasque in downtown L.A.

I'd also worked out a street route so

that if Curtis left me at traffic lights or at an intersection I could pick him up again. Like I said I was expecting a quiet evening. But one never knew. I finished off my cigarette and kept my eye on the big blue truck with the white stencil of the Maroc Trading Company on the sides and rear. It was the only blue-painted truck out within the next half-hour and Curtis had to be the driver.

It was just after half-eight when a big man in white coveralls came out the small wooden hut which served as an office. He shouted something to someone inside the door and then came around the rear end of the truck. He slid down the steel door and locked it. He went up to the cab and climbed aboard. He didn't look down in my direction. The diesel engine gunned up as he revved it. The gears ground and then the truck was picking its way across the uneven ground toward the gate.

I waited until he'd cleared the gate

and his mainbeams were a faint yellow pencil in the night before I started up the Buick and nosed down toward the main entrance. I stopped in front of the barrier as a man in a brown uniform with a revolver buckled round his waist came out the wooden hut. He peered briefly in the window at me. He had a tough, hard face with knowing eyes above a red nose and a black mustache.

"Mr Faraday? Mr Maltz said you'd be along about now."

He glanced away to the north toward the Baldwin Hills.

"We got a flash about half an hour ago. They're starting major roadworks tonight farther down. I'd follow that truck in if I was you. Save you half an hour, maybe."

I thanked the gateman. He went back in the hut and the barrier came up. He waved as I gunned on out. I didn't have much trouble keeping the truck in sight though Curtis was pushing her some. I soon saw what the gateman meant. About ten miles down the road lights were flashing and red-studded barriers were erected. Big yellow earth-moving machines were crawling under the arclights.

The blue-painted truck had already turned off to the right, on to a minor road that crawled up the hillside. I could see the red rear lights halfway up the bluff. I signalled and pulled the Buick over, the wheels rumbling over the rough surface of the secondary road and then her snout was pointed uphill to where the Maroc Trading Company vehicle was a faint scratch of red against the blue dimness of the hills.

I cut the headlights and dropped down my speed. There was just enough light to see the road-edge without making it dangerous and I didn't want to make my presence obvious to Curtis. His rear-lights died out round the far curve and I increased speed a little. I knew his destination but he might turn off or do something suspicious so

I didn't want to drop too far behind.

There was little traffic on this minor road which snaked its way up into the foothills and I only met two trucks coming in the opposite direction in half an hour. I'd picked up Curtis's lights again by now. The road went into a series of S-curves along the edge of a canyon and I could see the headlights from a mile away so I didn't hurry. I held the wheel with one hand and lit a cigarette with the other.

Curtis was maintaining a steady speed like most truckies and there were no more side roads which would take him into L.A. so I guess I wasn't paying as much attention as I might. A few minutes later I realised I'd lost the big blue truck. Then I picked up the yellow headlights again. There was the red and green neon of a big roadhouse way up ahead and I could see the lights pencilling up into a layby.

I slackened speed and waited until the signs drifted nearer in my windshield. It was a big place called Arcadi's. The road split into a layby each side and there were two wings from the laybys which made a horse-shoe to meet the main restaurant buildings. There were about thirty automobiles parked out front and quite a few trucks along the verge each side.

The Buick's tyres crunched over gravel as I pulled her off the road. I got in behind a big articulated truck at the far end and killed the motor. I doused the sidelights and got out, making sure I closed the door quietly. I could still hear the juddering mumble of Curtis's truck up ahead and faintly above it the noise of dance music coming from Arcadi's.

Then Curtis cut the motor and the chirping of cicadas and the faint soughing of wind in the treetops came back. The lights and smog of L.A. powdered the basin up ahead and reflected back off the horizon as I gum-shoed my way down between the trucks. I saw the rear lights of the Maroc Trading Company truck

84

go out. Nothing else happened for a minute or two.

Then I saw the glow of a torch near the cab. I stayed where I was behind the tailboard of a fruit lorry. The pale disc of Curtis's torch steadied down near the ground like he was studying the wheels of the vehicle. Then there came the rumble of wood on wood followed by the clink of metal. A regular tapping noise began. I waited to make sure. Curtis was changing a tyre on his rear wheel. I went back to the Buick, got in and lit another cigarette.

I switched on the dash light and looked at my watch. Already a quarter of an hour had crawled by. I got out the car again. The noise of the tyre-changing operation had stopped so I guessed Curtis had finished. I got up near the fruit truck before I heard the low mumble of conversation. I swore to myself. There was a big closed car with dark coachwork parked some way beyond Curtis's truck now. It certainly hadn't been there when we came in.

I couldn't see Curtis for a moment. Then I heard the sharp impact of steel on steel. The body of the truck was tilting. A tall figure got upright alongside the truck and shadows fled along the ground toward the red and green of the neon. A cry of pain and terror grew until it seemed to fill the whole night. I pounded up toward the truck as the big sedan gunned out. There were no lights on it and it swerved erratically until the driver hit the switch and the yellow pencils of the headlights stabbed at the trees lining the driveway.

The automobile went away fast, the tyres squealing shrilly until it straightened before bouncing back on to the main stem and dwindling in the direction of L.A. The scream had stopped now, was replaced by the hoarse exhalation of tortured breath. Then that sound too died and the noises of the night came back.

I stepped around the rear of the

Maroc truck. The big steel bar that the tall man had used to smash away the jack from under its body was lying at an angle and I almost fell over it.

Something was lying pinned by the truck body to the ground. Something in white coveralls now crushed and crawling with dark shadows. Something that only a few seconds earlier had been a man. I bent lower, fighting to prevent myself retching. A final bubble of expelled air from the dead man's lungs made a sharp hissing noise in the semi-darkness.

A black shadow wriggled from the mouth to join the splashes on the coveralls. The legs were still trembling. I got up. There was nothing anyone could do. Curtis had been a dead man the second the weight of the truck hit him. I got back to the Buick as quickly as I could. There was no-one else around. I felt my heart beating slightly faster than normal. You're getting old, Faraday, I told myself. I tell myself that at least twice on every case.

This looked like being a heavy one. I decided to carry the Smith-Wesson from now on in. I switched on the ignition and gunned down the layby. I waited for a gap in the traffic and then slotted in. I was nearly a hundred yards from Arcadi's before I switched on my main beam. I looked at the delivery list Maltz had given me, holding it under the dash-light.

This was one hell of a mess whichever way I looked at it. I would have to tell Maltz I'd lost Curtis and gone straight in to L.A. I couldn't afford to tangle with the L.A. Police this early on my inquiry. Someone was keeping tabs on me too. No sense in tipping my hand. I started making time in to L.A.

★ ★ ★

La Boutique Fantasque was a big place with mock Georgian windows, white painted and set in the middle of a large block of brick-fronted buildings in one of the business sections. There were lights burning in rear so I drove on past and found a place to park about two blocks farther down. I gum-shoed back along the street, keeping my eyes peeled. There was the smell of hot concrete and flowers and the traffic that went by, white-wall tyres shirring over the tarmac, set swirls of paper and cigarette foil dancing dustily in the polluted air.

I stepped off the sidewalk and crossed to the other side of the street. I cruised down, watching the façade opposite and noting the lay-out. There was an alley about a hundred yards down, which presumably led to a servicing area. That might be useful if I couldn't get in the front way. I didn't know why I'd come here. It was just a hunch really. Most of my work is. That and the fact that the toy shop was the first call on Curtis's list.

And the people who'd killed Curtis might be still around. They hadn't wanted his load, that was for sure. And Curtis must have met someone by arrangement. The tyre-changing bit was probably the pretext. But why kill him at all? Because they knew I was trailing him? The more I thought about it the screwier it became. And the more I didn't like it.

I finished my prowl at last and crossed over again, this time about three hundred yards away and on the same side as the shop. There were lights on in most of the windows along the boulevard and quite a few people about on the sidewalks. What I was looking for was characters seated in parked cars. I couldn't see any. But that didn't mean there weren't any around.

I slackened pace and started looking in the windows, using the glass to scrutinise the street behind me. I took fifteen minutes to cover the distance between me and the shop. I didn't see anything suspicious. But that still didn't mean anything. I grinned at my reflection in the glass in front of me. I was starting to take plastic

Donald Ducks seriously. I was up to La Boutique Fantasque now. The place was bigger than I thought.

It lived up to its name all right. There were toys of every shape, kind and size on shelves, in show cases and on the counters. There were beautifully painted model soldiers; mechanical men that walked; penguins poised on a slope above a miniature pool; railways; automobiles; and gigantic soft toys of the kind you don't often see today. I got in a darkened patch between the two windows and thought things out.

I lit a cigarette, cupping my hands to shield the glow. All the while I was searching the illuminated portion of the window in front of me, watching the reflections of the people who passed on the sidewalk. I still couldn't see anything suspicious. Maybe the whole thing was a crazy pipedream. I moved forward and tried the front door of the shop. It was locked, like I expected.

I went down the block and turned into the small alley that led in rear.

There were overhead lights set on brackets screwed to the brick wall of the building and there were no patches of shadow. Nothing moved in the whole stretch of tarmac. I went on down for about a hundred yards. The block ended then and there was a small service road with garages opposite. There were no automobiles around. I stood and smoked and finished off my cigarette and ground the butt beneath my heel.

Then I went down along in rear of the building, walking quietly, my movements masked by the dancing shadows of tree branches the low-key lighting was throwing on the ground. I passed four or five premises and stopped in the shadow of a doorway. La Boutique Fantasque had a corresponding show window this side of the building and light was spilling across the paving. There was a big white door with a brass handle which had DELIVERY ENTRANCE stencilled on it in black paint.

I waited three minutes until I'd satisfied myself there was no one within earshot. Then I eased forward into the lit area. The window was full of stuff; in fact, it was almost a replica of the ones which faced the street. But beyond was a storeroom with white-painted walls. Cartons like I'd seen in Troon's place were stacked from floor to ceiling. I went over and tried the door. It was unlocked. Ratchets started revolving in my head. Something didn't sit right about this.

I eased into the storeroom and quietly closed the door behind me. It had a Yale lock and I simply drew it to, to secure it. I lit another cigarette and looked around. The storeroom was an ordinary sort of place and it was obviously empty. But I never do anything in a hurry. In any case I was on enclosed premises without permission and I didn't want to lose my licence. And if the beatman caught me I could draw a term for breaking.

I crossed over from the door and went

behind a pile of boxes where I couldn't be seen through the window. Some of the cartons were open. I could see a selection of the mechanical penguins that were Troon's speciality. A giraffe's head protruded from another carton. And there were several stacks of the plastic Donald Ducks. I took one out of a case and examined it. Despite its flimsy look it was solidly made. I got hold of the neck and twisted.

It appeared to be all in one piece. Leastways, I couldn't shift it. I put the toy back exactly as I'd found it and eased my way down toward a door. It was already standing ajar. I peeked through. The place was half office, half showroom. There were white-painted room dividers full of mechanical and other toys; mirrors that made the place look twice as big; a large desk, a couple of swivel chairs and some filing cabinets.

I stood in the doorway smoking and sizing up the layout. Through the spaces of the room dividers I could see the main showroom and the sidewalk beyond. There didn't appear to be any living quarters or anything that looked like stairs leading up. There were a couple of plastic Donald Duck toys lying on the desk. There was something different about them.

Then I saw the head of one was off and lying on the blotter alongside. I moved forward and picked the head up. I saw it had a thread cut so it could be screwed back on to the body. There was something wrapped in plastic stuffed into the body of the duck.

I leaned over. That was when I saw a foot sticking out the other side of the desk. It had a blue suede shoe on it. A big man was laying on the polished board floor on the side away from me. He had a bearded face to match his body and his eyes were wide open in surprise. There was a lot of blood on his shirt-front. From the thin slit in the silk I would have figured a knife-wound.

I didn't have time to find out. I was just bending over to examine him when a ten-ton truck fell on my head and I went out in a crescendo of exploding sky-rockets.

8

A THIN wailing sound split my consciousness. It seemed to split my head too. I sat up, tasted blood. The room focused up. I was still lying in the back-room of La Boutique Fantasque. There was something different about the place though.

I couldn't make it out for the moment. I got up, almost retched. I sat with my back against the desk. The room was still dancing around me. Someone in steel-studded boots was doing a clog-dance on my skull. I closed my eyes and waited for the sickness to go away. I could smell burning. I opened my eyes again. My half-smoked cigarette was lying on the carpet in front of me.

I reached over and stubbed it out. It took me about a minute because I couldn't control my hands properly. I closed my eyes and reached in my pocket. I found my pack of cigarettes and put the half-smoked stub in it. I opened my eyes again and clawed myself up, holding on to the desk. The room was still spinning but some of the sickness was receding.

I swallowed bile and perspiration was cascading down my cheeks. I reached up with my right hand and felt the bump behind my ear. Whoever sapped me must have been standing to my left and about three feet behind. He couldn't have come in the door I'd used or I'd have seen him. Which meant he was already there. He had to be, of course, because he was the same character who'd knifed the bearded man on the floor. I started to laugh then. That showed how addled my brain processes had become. It seemed one hell of a joke for a minute.

I went over to the other side of the office where the mirrors were. I found a small wash-basin and rinsed my face.

I looked at my watch. It was almost eleven so I'd been out nearly half an hour. I stepped around the desk, stopped. There was no sign of the bearded man on the floor. I shook my head. Some of the mist cleared from my eyes. I got down and examined the boards. I soon found the dragging marks made by the dead man's heels.

I followed them over to the storeroom in rear. They disappeared out through the door. I snubbed the catch on the lock. I knew I wouldn't have any luck there. I went back into the office and looked around. The plastic ducks off the desk top had gone too. Someone had done a nice tidy job while I was out. Obviously the same people who'd fixed Curtis. Why, I didn't know. But it had to be something important for this.

And they'd left me to take the rap for a minor break-in. I guessed the bearded man had been the proprietor of La Boutique Fantasque. If he later turned up I'd get the blame for that too. I had no doubt he was dead. I'd seen too many corpses to make a mistake. None of it made any sense to me. But then I hadn't got any of the pieces yet. They could have killed me too while they were at it. I gave it up.

The wailing sound in the distance went on. It was a police siren. I hadn't got long. I went through the desk drawers. I didn't know what I was looking for. There was a large brown envelope in the second compartment down. The drawer was locked but the key was still in the lock. I saw there were some papers in the envelope. I stuffed it in the inside pocket of my jacket.

It wasn't much for an evening's work but that's the way it goes sometimes. I turned off the light in the office, dusting the switch with my handkerchief. The siren had cut out now. I reached the rear door of the shop when I heard the squealing of brakes in the alley. I got down and looked through the window.

The display lights gleamed on the blue bonnet of a patrol car.

There came a pounding on the front door at the same time. I got back in the dark of the office. There were two patrolmen trying the glass front entrance door. They shaded their eyes as they tried to look into the darkness beyond the showroom.

"Doesn't seem to be anything wrong," the bigger cop said. "Probably a false alarm."

"We'll go around in rear to make sure," the other one said.

Their silhouettes disappeared along the sidewalk. I waited perhaps thirty seconds until there came a pounding at the rear door. I got up then and walked down the short flight of steps into the showroom. I was sweating and I felt like an unknown actor turning up for the first day's work on a film set. There was an automatic lock on the front door. I clicked it back, stepped through on to the sidewalk and closed the door behind me.

I went along the front of the building trying hard not to run. There was another siren going now and as I got beyond the lighted area a third police automobile pulled in to the kerb. I walked two blocks and found a diner and got outside two cups of black coffee and waited until the hubbub had died down.

When I came out the throbbing in my head had started again. I could see red lights winking on top of the police automobiles in front of the shop. There was a cluster of people on the pavement outside. I wondered for a minute if they'd found the bearded man's body. I hoped I hadn't dropped anything around the premises. I'd wiped off with my handkerchief anything on which I could have left prints.

But in the state I'd been in when I came around I couldn't be sure. I'd know soon enough anyway. The police would be over at Park West if they knew anything. But I figured whoever had dropped the bearded man

102

had moved him. Because he might be connected with Curtis? And that would link him with the plastic toys and whatever they were being filled with?

I was in no condition for Einsteinian logic tonight. I turned back from the diner and skirted the area. I walked two blocks and then turned again, approaching the Buick in a huge circle. It was still where I'd parked it. There was no-one suspicious on the sidewalk though I waited a couple of minutes. I got behind the wheel, started the motor and tooled across town.

My headache felt worse by the time I got to Stella's place. I thumbed the bell twice. The door was just opening when I passed out for the second time in one evening.

* * *

The gold disc of Stella's hair shimmered into focus. She looked anxious. She moved the cold compress on my forehead. I stirred on the divan, tried to get up. Stella pushed me back. "You must have a skull like solid ivory, Mike," she said. "I ought to call a doctor."

"I'll be all right," I said.

Stella still looked dubious.

She wore a gold-coloured sweater and tailored slacks to match. Any other evening it would have sent my blood-count up. Tonight it only slightly raised my temperature. That showed how beat-up I was. I pushed Stella's hand gently away and started easing myself forward on the divan. My head swam and I sat back quickly. Stella got up, leaving the compress where it was. She had a strange look on her face.

"It might be fractured, Mike," she said.

"I'll get the doc to have a look at it in the morning," I said. "Right now I could use some coffee."

"Coming," Stella said.

She went out into the kitchen while I sat focusing up her living room. I'd only been in her apartment a couple of times before and tonight's visit still seemed like a novelty. I closed my eyes again and held the compress tightly against my forehead. The throbbing was going away now and the sickness had receded. Stella came back again and put the plastic beaker full of steaming liquid down on the table in front of the divan.

I got my legs on to the carpet and leaned forward. I was seeing sharply and clearly now. I kept the compress on while I sipped the brew.

"How did you get me on the divan?" I said.

"I've been trying to get you on the divan for years," Stella said.

I ignored that one.

"You must have had some help," I said.

"It wasn't easy," Stella admitted. "I knew those evening judo classes would come in useful. You want to tell me about it or save it for tomorrow?"

"I found a couple of stiffs tonight," I said. "Then someone topped me."

Stella nodded.

"Certainly some anti-social people around town," she said.

Her blue eyes looked at me expressionlessly. Stella was pretty good at playing down situations. Tonight she was surpassing herself.

"Looks like Faraday Investigations is going too deep, Mike."

"Faraday Investigations is firmly on the ball," I said.

I held out the beaker toward her. Stella grinned suddenly and the worry had gone from her eyes.

"All the while you can drink coffee, there's nothing much wrong," she said.

She went back in the kitchen again. I got up while she was doing that and prowled around. I was feeling more normal by the minute. I went over to the mantelpiece. There was a picture of myself and Stella in a hardwood frame. We were standing on the deck of her small sailing yacht Dulcibella. I was squinting into the sun and looked something like a cross

106

between Captain Ahab and Charlie Ruggles. Stella looked great. But then she always does.

She was back at my elbow. She put the beaker into my hand. Her eyes explored my face.

"That's a private picture, Mike," she said.

"I was only looking at it," I said.

Stella smiled enigmatically and went back over to the divan. She patted it like I was a pet dog or something. I went on over and sat down anyway. I was in no mood for argument tonight. Stella had a notebook and pencil out.

"You surely don't want a rundown now?" I said.

"Why not?" Stella said calmly. "That's what you pay me for. I'll get in the office early in the morning. You can see the doc and come in later."

"Thank you, Nurse Dugdale," I said.

I settled back on the divan and closed my eyes and gave Stella a rundown on the day's events in between sips of the scalding hot coffee. I was feeling better by the minute. Stella was silent for a moment as I finished. She'd covered five pages of her scratchpad with her shorthand notes.

"You'd best carry a gun from now on in, Mike," she said.

"It hadn't escaped my attention," I said.

Stella leaned back on the divan and cupped her palms round her right knee. She frowned as she rocked to and fro.

"Albert Troon won't be pleased," she said.

"About Curtis? You'd better ring him."

"What's the story?" Stella said.

"I lost him on the way in to L.A.," I said. "I waited for him at an intersection but he didn't turn up. I don't want the police linking me with the kill."

I opened my eyes and put the beaker back on the table. Stella watched me for a moment without saying anything.

"Troon won't give you a very high rating," she said.

"That worries me a lot," I said.
"You'd better check in the morning and find out who owns La Boutique Fantasque. If it's a big man with a beard then we got something."

Stella wrinkled up her forehead.

"Why would anybody want to remove the corpse?" she said. "Or put packages in hollowed-out Donald Ducks, for that matter?"

"That's why we're in business, honey," I said.

I got out my package of cigarettes and looked at her.

"You oughtn't to smoke, Mike," she said. "It'll only bring back your headache."

I put the pack back in my pocket. Maybe she was right at that. I took the compress down from my forehead and stared over to the far wall to where a mass of anodised steel rods hung. I was still trying to read some significance into them when I left.

"Maybe the killers didn't want the shop turned over," I said. "So they took the body away."

Stella looked at me with that maddeningly sure expression of hers.

"You haven't explained why they wanted to kill him in the first place."

"You can't have everything," I said. "Probably because the shop owner was doing something on the premises they needed to cover up."

"Because you might find out?" Stella said.

She sat back and cupped her other knee.

"What do you think was in the package, Mike. Drugs?"

"Could be," I said. "That might be a likely explanation. But it would have to be consignments worth millions of dollars to warrant suck a high death-rate. Two in two hours is going some."

"Even for you," Stella said.

She had a good point there. I sat nursing my beaker of coffee and trying to paste my thoughts together. I wasn't making a very good job of it so I gave it up for tonight. Stella came to the door with me. Her lips felt warm and yielding against my face. She put cool finger-tips up and ran them along the angle of my jaw.

"Take care, Mike."

"Sure," I said. "Isn't that what I'm always doing? And thanks for the cosmetic surgery."

Stella was still smiling as the door cut her off from my sight. I went down to ground level and back to the Buick. The night was quiet and still and there was no-one around in this section of town. Unless you counted the traffic passing on the main stem and a plane somewhere out in the haze circling L.A. International Airport. But one got used to those things. For L.A. it was pretty quiet.

I was just reaching open the door of the Buick when a light flared somewhere and the street was like midday. A fat man just coming out the vestibule of Stella's apartment block blinked in the glare. I looked up. There was a big ball of fire in the sky above

L.A. It burned white hot for perhaps four or five seconds. The dull boom of an explosion followed, slapping echoes off the hills.

The aircraft noise had stopped and fragments of blazing material went snaking toward the ground. They made little red and yellow patterns in the night sky. They seemed to take a long time to reach the ground. The lights were about six or seven miles away I should have said.

There were a lot of people in the street now, shading their eyes and looking off toward the airport. They seemed to have come from out the ground. A siren started up somewhere, faint and far away. The big ball of fire had disappeared but burning pieces were still coming down. There were fires on the ground now and a second siren had joined the first.

"Christ!" the fat man said. "That was a big one."

He turned to me like the shock was still in his eyes.

"Looks like it," I said.

I got in the Buick and closed the door. I could still see the glow of reflected flame in the far distance of the night. It was pink and blue now. I could imagine the stink of kerosene and the panic at the airport. I'd seen too many in the past few years. Some people were running for their automobiles. I could already see the choked-up highways leading to the area. Ghouls always came out the woodwork whenever there was a disaster. The fat man's face was framed in my driving window.

"They can't have had a chance," he breathed.

I looked at my wrist-watch. It was past one a.m. The fat man inclined his head.

"You going out there?" he said. "I wondered if I could grab a lift . . . "

I shook my head. "They won't get any deader," I said.

The fat man grinned.

"Too true, brother, but I sure would

113

like to see that wreck. I sort of collect disasters."

"You'll have to collect them without my help," I said.

The fat man creased up his face again.

"Life must go on," he said brightly.

He scuttled away to the far kerb where a family were piling into a station wagon. I gunned out and went on home to bed. I figured I'd had enough for one day.

9

I SAT in the breakfast nook of my Park West House and worked my way through my third piece of toast and pineapple. My head felt about normal size and I figured I could get across town to the doc's without falling apart. I'd just switched on the radio and the eight a.m. bulletin was coming through on one of the local stations.

I'd broken out my favourite Smith-Wesson .38 with the short barrel from the small armoury I kept in a locked cupboard in my bedroom and the bulk of the gun in the webbing holster under my arm made a comforting pressure against my muscles as I moved. The air crash was the third item. Apparently a Tri-Star had blown up on circling to land at L.A. International. Over a hundred people had died and of

115

those in hospital several more weren't expected to recover. It didn't make very good breakfast listening.

It seemed pretty obvious an explosion aboard the aircraft was involved but apparently there was more to it than that. There'd been several Arabs among the passengers, the bulletin went on. The wreckage was still being sifted for evidence but one of the theories was that terrorists among the passengers were carrying an explosive device which had exploded prematurely. The Arab passengers were among the dead so it was only a theory for the moment.

I flipped off the switch and went on with my breakfast. I was just finishing when the phone buzzed. I got out the breakfast nook and went over to the extension. It was Stella.

"Just wondered how the head was?"

"Back to normal size," I said.

Stella made a clicking noise with her tongue.

"Look in at the doc's just the same," she said.

116

"On my way over," I told her.

I put down the phone and went round the house locking up. A fine drizzle was falling, coating the sidewalk with a greasy-looking film. I got the Buick out the carport and eased my way across town. The traffic was pretty thick this time of morning. I'd already rung the doc so he was expecting me.

A thin, stringily-built man with a startling white shock of hair, he was good at his job. He probed around with his fingers at my skull and grunted occasionally. He sat down at his desk and scratched moodily on a pad.

"You've had mild concussion," he said at last. "Effect mostly worn off but I'd take it easy for a day or two. No fracture. You may get a headache or two in the next week."

He pushed his glasses up over the bridge of his nose and looked at me quizzically.

"You don't want to tell me about it?"

"Nothing to tell," I said, buttoning

117

my shirt and moving away from the X-ray machine. "I fell down the rear steps over at my house."

Drexel made a faint derisive noise back in his throat.

"That's for the record," he said. "This is me you're talking to. I've seen too many blows like this. Somebody sapped you."

I grinned.

"Put it down in your records as a fall, anyway, doc." I said. "You're not the only one tight-lipped about his business affairs."

Drexel rumpled his thatch of white hair and tore off a prescription from his pad. Little sparks of humour were glinting in back of his faded blue eyes. He tossed the sheet over to me.

"Go get this filled, anyway. I guess I'll just have to read about it in the paper."

"You will at that, doc," I said.

I thanked him and went on out. I walked a block to a drug-store and got the prescription filled. The druggist had some difficulty in reading Drexel's tortured script and had to ring him back. That took another fifteen minutes. By the time I got back in the Buick it was a quarter of ten and I didn't reach the office until a quarter past. I rode up in the creaking elevator and went down the familiar corridor. I could hear Stella's typewriter pecking a hundred feet away.

★ ★ ★

I heard her cross to the alcove before I got the waiting room door open. I grinned. I took off my raincoat and made myself comfortable at my old broadtop.

"Make it plenty hot," I said.

Stella peeked out from behind the glass-screen and smiled. It looked really something.

"How's the old beat-up character this morning?"

"Just as beat-up," I said. "I went to see Drexel. Nothing more than mild

119

concussion. Nothing that a couple of days' rest and a slug of this won't cure."

I pushed over the bottle the druggist had made up for me. Stella uncorked it and sniffed at it cautiously.

"Do you drink it or use it as an embrocation?" she said.

"It certainly smells like horse liniment," I said.

Stella came back with a spoon and a tooth-glass. She measured out the required quantity and gave it me to drink. It tasted pretty vile but the coffee would soon get rid of that. I sat back and put my feet up and closed my eyes while Stella finished making the brew. I didn't come to life again until she waved the cup underneath my nose.

"I got hold of Troon at home," Stella said. "He nearly had apoplexy."

"Sore?" I said.

Stella shook her head.

"More shocked. I gave him your message. He wasn't anxious to have the police gumming up his factory. He said he'd co-operate and that he wasn't keen to advertise that he'd had to call on outside help."

I sipped the first drops of coffee and looked over to where a faint shaft of sunlight was penetrating the vaporous haze that hung over the boulevard outside. I turned back to Stella and put the coffee down on my blotter. She carried her own cup over to her desk and sat facing me.

"He sounds a sensible man," I said. "About what I figured."

Stella nodded.

"He told me to tell you he trusted you and that he'd wait until you got in touch."

"Even more sensible," I said. "What about La Boutique Fantasque?"

"I already checked," Stella said.

I put down my cup.

"Christ," I said. "I wasn't that serious."

"Faraday Investigations never sleep," Stella said.

"Only the principal," I said, fingering

121

the bump on the back of my head.

I slammed the cork tight on the bottle of fizzwater Doc Drexel had prescribed and put it in a drawer of my desk. Stella looked at me in that maddeningly imperturbable manner she has.

"Don't you want to know about Alex Kinross?"

"Don't bring any more people in," I said. "With the state of my head I can't cope with the ones I've got."

"He owns the toyshop," Stella said.

She sat with her hands round her coffee cup and frowned at the rain starring the window panes.

"So?" I said.

"So I rang the Chamber of Commerce," Stella said. "I happen to have a good friend there."

"Naturally," I said.

Stella smiled faintly and picked up her cup again. I waited for her to go on.

"I was discreet, of course. I said a friend wanted to buy some unusual mechanical toys for her children.

Kinross's name came up in the conversation."

"Where does that get us?" I said.

"If you'll have patience I'll tell you."

There was a faint note of asperity in Stella's voice. I picked up my spoon and stirred the depths of my cup. A single shaft of sunlight spilled through the window and made shifting patterns on the surface of the coffee.

"Anyway, I called in there on my way to work."

I looked at Stella thoughtfully.

"They start early at the Chamber these days."

"They opened up specially for me," Stella said.

"He must be a good friend," I said.

Stella ignored that.

"I looked through their Directory," she went on. "I also had a look at the register. Kinross has been running the place about six years. They had a photograph in their file. I got a Xerox copy."

She took an envelope out of her

handbag and flipped it over to me. I opened it up. Like all photo-copies it wasn't a good likeness. The picture was of a plump man with a beard. So far as I could tell it was the same character I'd seen lying on the floor last night giving a first-class imitation of a corpse.

"Good girl," I said.

I passed the envelope back to Stella and sat on, sipping my coffee.

"Check?" she said.

"I think it's the same character," I told her. "Which reminds me, I ought to look over there again today. If Kinross is still missing, his absence should cause some comment."

Stella's smile was a degree wider now.

"I've been on to the shop," she said. "A man's voice answered. I made an inquiry and rang off."

I looked at Stella for a moment in silence.

"My presence in this organisation hardly seems necessary," I told the filing cabinet.

I emptied my cup and sat back in my swivel chair.

"So Kinross may be still missing. In which case the character at the shop now might know something."

"Or if Kinross is back he wasn't dead last night and knows who slugged you," Stella finished for me.

"It needs a careful touch," I said.

"You want me to go on over?" Stella asked.

I shook my head.

"They know me already so it won't hurt to go back again. I might need you for later."

"That's nice to know," Stella said. She got up and collected the cups and took them back to the alcove. I leaned forward in the chair when I heard a crackling noise. I reached in my inside pocket and drew out a brown envelope. I was still sitting looking at it when Stella came back.

"That bump really must have jolted my cogs last night," I said. "I took this from Kinross's desk. I'd clean forgotten about it until now."

Stella came and stood by the desk, looking down at the envelope. She didn't say anything. I opened up the flap and took the contents out. There were three sheets of paper inside. They looked like photocopies, the detail grey, the surface an unmistakable photographic texture. The first two pages were mathematical formulae. I looked up from the sets of figures at Stella. She was frowning.

"They're Greek to me, too, Mike," she said.

I turned up the third sheet. The paper was covered with symbols that looked like some sort of wiring diagram. Long lines joined up in angular formal patterns to square boxes. There were letters on the diagram, from A to L. I shut my eyes and pushed the stuff away from me.

"Very revealing," I said.

"It might be important, Mike," Stella said.

She gathered up the papers and

returned them to the envelope.

"I'll put these in the safe."

"File them under U while you're at it," I said. "Useless."

I got up and went over to the window. The pain was gone from my head and I felt normal again. I looked out at the boulevard. It seemed like the rain had stopped now.

"Did you hear that smash last night?" I said. "When the jet came down?"

Stella shook her head. "I had the radio on just after you left. They had a bulletin. An awful thing. Why did you ask?"

"I just wondered," I told her. "I saw it come down. I was just getting into the car outside your apartment."

Stella went over, eased on to her desk and sat swinging long legs.

"Are we lunching together?" she said.

"If I can get back in time," I said. "I'm going over to the toyshop. Don't wait if I'm not back by one."

I went out and rode down in the

elevator. The rain had stopped so I carried my waterproof over my arm. I picked up the Buick from my usual garage and drove across town. I put the radio on to get the latest bulletin. They were still going on about the jet crash. I almost ran into the back of a truck. I stamped on the brake and swore. A traffic cop, his slicker gleaming with moisture scowled in my direction.

The bulletin-reader went on, his bland expressionless tones clear above the throb of the engine; "Vital clues to the crash for the investigators and almost certainly the seat of the explosion, are fragments of yellow plastic which have now been identified as a child's toy duck."

10

I OPENED the door of La Boutique Fantasque and went on in over the polished wood floor toward the staircase at the rear of the shop. There was no bell and I was trying not to make too much noise. I stopped on the lower level of the salon and pretended to admire a set of mechanical soldiers which were set up in open order drill formation. There was a shuffling noise going on in rear and something that sounded like drawers being opened and shut.

I shifted over quietly until I could see through the openwork dividers into the office area where I'd been last night. A tall man in a well cut light brown suit was standing with his back to me. From where I was it sounded like he was swearing to himself under his breath. I grinned and stepped closer.

There didn't seem to be anyone else around.

The big man went along the dividers and rummaged around some more. Evidently he didn't find what he was looking for because he swore to himself again. He came back up the room. This time he was facing me but he had his eyes turned downward and he still didn't spot me on the floor of the shop.

He was about thirty-five and had smooth black hair that was combed straight back in a thick mass from his forehead. He had a wide, high forehead and his eyes, under sandy brows, were brown. Right now they looked angry and he kept biting his lips. He had a tight, bitter mouth that spoilt the regularity of his features and made his face look mean and a small triangular white scar at the right-hand corner of his lips.

He had a mauve silk bow-tie hanging under the collar points of his cream shirt and something I hadn't seen for a long time; a vee-necked pullover worn under his jacket. It made him look like Patric Knowles in a thirties movie. Except that Patric Knowles was much better looking. He had a mauve silk handkerchief to match the bow-tie peeking from the breast pocket of his jacket. I didn't take to him.

I'd just made up my mind about that when he shifted position. He went over toward the desks and started opening and shutting the drawers in a sort of controlled frenzy. He stood up again, his face white with fury. It was about then that he spotted me. He gave a violent start and took a step backwards like I was threatening him.

"Find what you're looking for?" I said.

The big man started again. He looked blank. It took him a full five seconds to recover himself. He attempted to smile, made a rotten job of it. He waved a hand in the air to indicate the jumbled state of the office behind him.

"We had a break-in last evening. The

police have been here half the night. That's why I'm upside down."

"Sorry to hear that," I said. "Anything valuable taken?"

The big man gave me a hard look. He moved over and then came down the little staircase toward me.

"What makes you say that?" he said in an equally hard voice.

"The way you were turning those drawers over I figured you might have lost something important," I said.

The big man's face looked as if a whiplash had just been flicked across it.

"Just checking," he said. "I shan't know what's missing until I've gone through everything."

"Did they catch him?" I said.

The big man shook his head slowly. He was on the main floor of the shop now and he looked suddenly vulnerable and tired, despite his solidity.

"Hard luck," I said.

"I didn't get your name . . . " he said.

"I didn't give it," I told him. "I'm looking for Mr Kinross, really. He's the proprietor, I believe."

The tall man inclined his head.

"Unfortunately, you've chosen a bad time. Mr Kinross is away on his annual holidays. Perhaps I can help you?"

"Possibly," I said.

I waited and the tall man was the first to break the silence.

"I'm sorry," he said, holding out a lean, damp hand for me to shake. "I'm Rudolph Mayer, Mr Kinross's manager. I'm as au fait with the business as he, so if you'll tell me what you want . . ."

"My name's Parker," I said, interrupting him. "It's a purely personal matter, really. I don't know anything about toys."

Mayer looked disappointed. There was a curious baffled expression in his eyes.

"When are you expecting Mr Kinross back?" I said.

Mayer bit his lip. It was quite a habit with him.

"In about three weeks' time," he said quickly. "I believe he's moving around."

"So he didn't leave any forwarding address," I said.

Mayer shook his head.

"I regret not," he said. "But if it's urgent . . . "

"It will have to wait," I said.

★ ★ ★

Mayer put on his baffled look again. He seemed only to have about three basic expressions. I guessed it wasn't his day. I decided to prolong the agony a bit. He was standing looking at me with his hands at his sides and his fists balled like he didn't know whether to lose control of himself or break into a soft-shoe dance. I decided to save him the trouble.

"However, now that I'm here, I may as well have a look around," I said.

I moved forward. Mayer gave ground before me.

"Fascinating place you have here," I said.

I passed Mayer and started up the small staircase that led to the office.

"Did you realise there's a lot of stuff on the floor up here?" I called down.

Mayer came bounding up toward me. He had difficulty keeping control. There was a scowl on his face but he tried to change it into a smile. It wasn't a success.

"No-one's allowed up here," he said. "This is a private office. I told you we had a break-in."

"I'm sorry," I said. "I didn't mean to intrude. Can I help in clearing up the mess?"

Mayer looked at me suspiciously.

"I can manage all right, Mr Parker," he said. "Just so long as I'm left alone."

I was beginning to enjoy myself by now. I started back down the staircase again.

"You carry on," I said. "I'll just

135

rummage about. If you want any help just call."

Mayer swallowed. Hectic red spots were beginning to burn on both cheeks.

"It's really very good of you, Mr Parker, but I can manage."

He had a problem getting the words out in a civil tone.

"We must all try and help one another, Mr Mayer," I said. "It's a difficult world."

I moved away and started going down the shelves, humming to myself and giving a pretty good imitation of a character who'd got all the time in the world. Mayer stood watching me for a moment or two longer. Then he squared his shoulders, appeared to get a grip on his nerves and went back in the office. I grinned to myself. I moved over to a stand which featured a ramp and a dozen or so of Troon's mechanical penguins.

They had the blue and gold cipher of the Maroc Trading Company stamped on their bases. I was still standing there when I became aware I was being watched. I knew Mayer had his eye on me, of course. He was in the office but I could sense rather than see his gaze on me in the mirrors over the washbasin area in the corner of the office. I still couldn't quite figure him.

He was acting jumpily but that could have been because of the break-in. Most normal people show signs of stress in unusual situations. The major question of course, was whether he'd been one of the characters who topped me the previous night. In which case he'd know I was on to him. Which would be more than enough to account for his jitters. It was an interesting question.

There was someone else in the place who was watching me closely too. Don't ask me how I knew. One gets an instinct about these things. And every instinct I possessed told me there was a second pair of eyes following me around. Most of the shop premises was open-plan. That meant someone was stationed in rear of the crates in the storeroom and giving me the eye.

Or else there was another room I didn't know about, fitted with a peep-hole or a two-way mirror. Perhaps over the washbasins. It didn't matter for the moment but I'd like to have known who it was. I'd have to keep my eyes peeled when I left.

I decided to give Mayer a lead. I shifted over and pretended to examine a pile of Troon's plastic Donald Ducks which were stacked in a pyramid on top of a showcase. If Mayer were what he seemed to be he might not react. If he did I could be on to something. I wouldn't be tipping my hand because I hadn't got a hand to tip. If an unknown third person in the shop were watching me he'd already know I'd been to the shop the night before. It was no chance either way.

The clatter as the pyramid of ducks went down brought Mayer out on to the staircase. He made a clucking noise deep in his throat as the bright yellow ducks bounced and rolled all over the showroom. I put on a contrite expression and spread out my arm.

"Do forgive me, Mr Mayer. Clumsy of me. I caught my coat-sleeve."

An unhappy look passed across Mayer's face. I almost felt sorry for him. I was already on my knees, picking up ducks and re-stacking them. I cautiously twisted the neck of the first duck I picked up. Mayer went white.

"What are you doing?" he squawked. He sounded like Donald Duck himself.

"I wondered if they came open," I said. "I thought I might get one for my small nephew and fill it with candy."

Mayer was looming over me now, his bulk blocking out the light from the windows.

"Whatever made you think that, Mr Parker?" he said in a curious voice.

"Nothing, really," I said, "except that most of these toys come apart."

The big man almost jumped in the

air as I twisted the neck of another duck.

"Be careful, you'll break them," he bellowed.

I looked at him sharply.

"They cost all of a dollar each," I said. "I'd be glad to make good any damage."

Mayer saw his mistake, tried to cover it up clumsily. He calmed down.

"It's just that Mr Kinross is so particular," he said sullenly.

He looked round the littered floor.

"I don't know what he'd say if he could see this."

"As he isn't here it hardly matters," I said, getting up and dusting off the knees of my trousers. I put two more ducks back on the pyramid. My eyes were searching the room still but I couldn't spot the silent watcher.

Mayer went over into a corner and rooted out two more ducks. He came back and poked them into the pyramid on top of the showcase with his thick, stubby fingers. He looked so vicious while he was doing this I figured the birds might fly off in alarm.

"This looks a great gadget," I said, picking up a large metal crane which had a working jib and a fully automated operator in the cab. The heavy hook on the end of the crane cable caught against a column of tin drums on another fitting, which began to totter. I thought Mayer was going to have a heart attack. He lunged forward to save the sagging pile. He was just in time.

"Do be careful, Mr Parker," he brayed. "I suppose you do intend to purchase something . . ."

He checked himself and bit his lip. Sweat was glistening on his forehead now. He turned almost guiltily as the showroom door opened and a trendy-looking young couple came in. The man had a broad-brimmed suede hat and a long cape which made him look like a late nineteenth-century artist. The girl was pretty nice and had a fringed buckskin outfit and plenty of bust and buttocks to go with it.

"You really must watch your nerves, Mr Mayer," I said. "You'll blow a gasket in a minute."

Mayer mumbled something under his breath and then had himself under control.

"I'm not myself today, Mr Parker," he muttered. "I've had a trying night."

"Sure, I understand," I told him. "Don't let me keep you from the cash customers."

Mayer looked at me hesitantly and then went on down the showroom to where the leggy girl in buckskin was enthusiastically winding up a doll that was almost lifesize. I waited a moment or two until he was well engaged in conversation. Then I went up the staircase quietly, making no noise.

I got through into the storeroom when I heard the outer door click softly. I grinned and came back toward the staircase. I looked down. Mayer hadn't noticed my temporary disappearance. I stood there for a moment longer. There was a faint, elusive perfume in the office now. It seemed familiar but I couldn't place it. I got back down on the showroom floor before Mayer turned around.

"I'll come again some time when Mr Kinross is back," I said.

"You do that, Mr Parker," Mayer said cheerily.

His eyes were focused somewhere beyond me like he was trying to erase the impression of my visit. The blonde girl in buckskins looked approvingly at me. The character from La Vie Bohème was up the other end of the showroom, crowing over Troon's mechanical soldiers. The girl blew me a kiss over Mayer's shoulder and bit her white teeth together provocatively.

"You and me both," I told her.

"I beg your pardon," Mayer said, startled.

"We got some crossed wires," I said, returning the girl's glance. "Perhaps I'll go see Mrs Kinross."

"Mr Kinross isn't married," said Mayer sharply.

"Lucky man," I said, still looking at the blonde girl.

I went out and left them all standing there. I picked up the Buick and drove across town. I just had time to take Stella for lunch.

11

THE offices of Dacey, Finch and Skidmore were on the second floor of an unpretentious granite building on a side-street in downtown L.A. I found a slot in which to park the Buick and walked in over an old-fashioned tiled paving in the lobby to an oak board which had the names of the firms situated in the building written in gold-painted curlicue script.

There was a hush in the place like it was a cathedral or something and people in dark clothes were creeping about. The sun was shining this afternoon but it still didn't give much light in here. I looked for the stained glass but I couldn't see any. They'd stopped just short of that.

I walked up a creaking staircase with heavy balustrades to the second floor. The corridor was covered in brown linoleum which smelt heavily of wax polish and the sober mahogany doors flanking the corridor had long-winded names on them. They all seemed to be lawyers or insurance companies. I sighed. I'd had enough of lawyers recently. It would be a change getting into insurance.

I found the door I wanted and knocked and went in like the notice on the panel said. Two nice-looking girls in sensible grey skirts and frilly blouses were making mumbling noises on their electric typewriters in rear of a polished oak balustrade. The brown linoleum in the corridor had crept in here too. The walls were pale primrose and hung with legal-looking certificates and documents. Two or three doors in rear opened off the main office.

One of the girls glided over to the balustrade and looked at me expectantly. She had glossy blonde hair that was parted straight in the middle and her blue eyes looked very appealing behind her horn-rimmed spectacles. I wasn't fooled by her nice-as-butter manner though. This sort of girl can be dynamite in the right situation. Or the wrong situation, come to that. I figured she was harmless enough in the office.

"Can I help you?" she said mildly.

"Sure," I said. "My name's Faraday. I'd like to see Mr Dacey."

The girl shook her head.

"He's very busy right now. Have you an appointment?"

I shook my head. The girl hesitated again. The other girl behind the balustrade had stopped stroking the green-painted machine in front of her and was watching us curiously.

"He's been out all night on the air-crash," the girl said dubiously.

"That's why I'm here," I said.

The girl ran a very pink tongue round her full lips.

"That's a different matter, Mr Faraday. I wouldn't disturb Mr Dacey normally under these circumstances. But I'll just go see."

I thanked her and waited while she went and tapped at one of the rear doors. The other girl smiled at me shyly and then started attacking her typewriter again. I didn't have long to wait. The blonde job with the glasses was back almost immediately.

"Mr Dacey will see you now, Mr Faraday."

She smiled mysteriously. "Mr Dacey's my father. That's why I'm so protective."

"Thanks for warning me," I said.

The girl smiled again and opened the door in the balustrade and let me through. I followed her in to the office in rear. It was a small room, about ten feet square, with white plastic blinds at the windows overlooking the boulevard. The available room was taken up by a desk and two big filing cabinets. Apart from that there were a few framed certificates on the walls, filing trays full of papers, a leather armchair for Dacey and two more chairs in front of the desk.

A big man with grey hair and a face

crumpled with fatigue was standing by the window looking down at the boulevard. He had a crumpled blue suit to match his face and wide, blue eyes that had a piercing glance. He had a strong, honest look about him that I liked immediately.

He came forward to shake hands with a dry, crushing grip. He was about fifty and his big, raw-boned face was red with sun and wind. He had a plastic beaker of steaming coffee in his left hand and he put it down on his desk now and looked at me and the girl without speaking for a moment. Then he waved me into a chair and went around the desk to sit down himself.

"Perhaps Mr Faraday would like some coffee too, Deirdre," he said.

"Try me," I said.

The girl smiled hesitantly at me.

"You'd better bring me another cup," Dacey said. "Then leave us alone, honey. I don't want to be disturbed for the next half hour."

He waited until the girl had gone out and then looked at me sharply. He pushed over a half empty package of cheroots.

"Smoke?"

"I'll use my own if you don't mind," I said.

Dacey picked up his coffee cup and drained it. Then he crushed the plastic in his big hands and threw it over his shoulder. It landed square in the waste paper basket. He hadn't even glanced at it. Dacey chuckled.

"Habit," he said. "I understand you want to see me about last night's smash. You must excuse my appearance. I've been out there most of the night and this morning."

"That's all right, Mr Dacey," I said. "I understand."

"The name's Tom," Dacey said, looking at me shrewdly. "No need to be formal."

The girl was back again now. She put down the beakers of coffee without a word and went out quietly, shutting

150

the door behind her. Dacey had her well-trained. I got out the photostat of my licence in the plastic holder and passed it over to him. He studied it frowningly for a moment and then passed it back without comment.

"I saw your name in today's paper," I said. "That's why I'm here."

"You interest me, Mr Faraday," he said.

I sat back in my chair and feathered blue smoke at the ceiling.

"You understand I've got to be discreet, Mr Dacey," I said.

The big man smiled.

"The name's still Tom," he said. "Looks like we're on the same wavelength. Discretion's my middle name."

"Just so long as we understand each other," I said. "I wouldn't like to go off half-cock on this thing."

Dacey picked up his second beaker of coffee and looked at me shrewdly.

"I understand something of the way you fellows work, Mike," he said. "I

151

work rather in the same way myself. You want to protect your sources, is that it?"

"Something like that," I said. "I don't want the official police in. Not for any shady reasons but because I work better that way. I figured we might help each other."

Dacey put down his beaker and stroked his chin with the big fingers of his right hand.

"We might," he said. "My report's confidential for the time being. But the authorities will have to know all you know eventually. If you know anything, that is . . . "

"I know something, Tom," I told him. "I want a week at least."

I picked up the beaker the girl had left and tasted the coffee. It was almost as good as Stella's.

Dacey's rumpled face was alive with interest now.

"I think we could manage a fortnight," he said.

"Good enough," I said. "I read in

the paper about a yellow plastic toy being at the seat of the explosion."

A heavy shadow passed across Dacey's face.

"That's another of the things I'm up against," he said moodily. "It's an important piece of evidence. It should have been kept quiet. But some officious fool in the police department had to give it out to the press. I think we can co-operate. You look like a fellow who can keep a tight mouth. What's your suggestion?"

"That we pool our knowledge," I said. "I'm on a case involving the theft of plastic toys from a factory in L.A. I've reason to believe this might be tied up with the explosion which wrecked the jet last night."

There was no sign of tiredness in Dacey's face now. He stood up and put his hand across the desk for me to shake.

"You got yourself a deal, Mike," he said.

12

THE office was blue with smoke. I was halfway through my third beaker of coffee and the girl Deirdre was sitting at my elbow taking notes. Dacey sat supporting his chin on his cupped hands as I told him my story. I'd cleaned it up a little but it was basically as it had happened. I was going out on a limb here but Dacey had already given his promise and I'd made up my mind that he was a man I could trust.

The girl said nothing but her eyes were wide and bright behind her glasses as she went on with her note-taking. She crossed her legs with a shirring of tights and smiled at me as she turned another page in her notebook. I stopped for breath and Dacey broke the silence for the first time.

"You took a chance coming here," he said.

"I take a chance every day in my business," I told him. "I learn to judge character quickly. I figured you for clean-limbed and solidly dependable."

Dacey grinned and the girl had a sudden fit of coughing. She looked at me appealingly over the handkerchief she clapped to her mouth.

"Solid is right," Dacey said. "We'd make a good team. You know you could lose your licence for what you just told me."

"I almost lose my licence every other case," I told him. "I couldn't operate if I turned every piece of information over to the police. We work together pretty well usually."

Dacey rubbed his thick hands together and picked up his cheroot again.

"Just read me back what you got so far, Deirdre," he said.

We both listened while the girl read out from her notes in a clipped, efficient-sounding voice. There were still traces of pink on her cheeks as she finished. She was a pretty good note-taker. I couldn't detect any errors in what I'd told her.

"You'd better type that up and bring it back to me in the confidential file," the big man said.

The girl got up and went out without looking at either of us. Dacey looked after her approvingly.

"Smart girl, that," he said. "Worth her weight in oil in a business like mine. Like you, I got to have someone I can trust absolutely."

He leaned back in his chair and puffed furiously at his cheroot.

"We got something here, Mr Faraday," he said, darting a sharp glance at me through the smoke. "I'm real grateful to you."

"It may be nothing," I said. "But over a hundred people died last night. And that's important."

Dacey inclined his head.

"I think we got a link all right. Two possible murders over shipments

156

of plastic toys. It's got to be something fantastic like this. Besides, I haven't told you everything yet. There was another explosion aboard a State Airlines jet two months ago. The same sort of toy was at the seat of the blast."

There was a long silence in the office.

"Many killed?" I said.

Dacey nodded. "Eighty-five," he said. "Plane blew up coming in to land at Montreal. Now this."

"What about the insurance?" I said.

Dacey ran his thumb along his chin. It was quite a habit with him.

"Millions of dollars," he said. "Takes a while to sort out. The last blast was from a plastic explosive packed into some sort of child's toy. I say that now but we didn't know at the time. Last night's explosion left bigger fragments and we were able to get an idea of the container. That's why your information is so important."

"What's this Arab angle?" I said.

Dacey got up and went over to one

of his file cabinets and rummaged around.

"There's a dossier here," he said. "That's on the Montreal disaster. Plus the passenger list. We haven't got the full list from last night's yet."

He put the file down on the desk in front of me and went around to his chair and sat down again. I picked up the cardboard folder and flipped over the typewritten sheets. I stopped on page three and turned back again. Dacey watched me with growing concentration.

"I see you had Arab passengers on that one," I said.

"It was put down to terrorist bombing," Dacey said. "The police and the other authorities called in thought the package had gone off too soon."

"Killing the Arabs as well," I said. "Pretty incompetent wasn't it?"

Dacey rubbed his chin again.

"Maybe they were using some new type of explosive which was unstable," he said. "How would I know? There've got to be a few foul-ups."

"Or an Israeli group might have been getting revenge?"

Dacey turned his tired blue eyes on me.

"I'd thought of that, Mike," he said. "We didn't get anywhere with it. And it isn't true to pattern. The Israelis haven't been going in for that sort of thing since the Middle East troubles began. Besides, we checked out the passengers pretty thoroughly. The Arab passengers were pretty obscure. Ordinary people, not government or politicals. Wouldn't be worth anybody's while to kill a hundred people to get three unimportant ones."

"It's a lousy world," I said.

"You can say that again," Dacey said.

He glanced at his wrist watch.

"We've got a lot to talk about," he said. "But right now I could do with some sack-time."

"Sure," I said. "I'll come back again."

"Deirdre will ring you if you leave the number," Dacey said. "And thanks for coming in. We'll work together just fine."

"Can I give you a lift?" I said.

Dacey shook his head.

"I'm bunking here for the time being," he said, indicating another doorway at the side of the office. "I use the divan in there when things get hot like now. Then I'm available."

I went on out and left him standing by the desk looking out over the boulevard like he was trying to read the answers to a lot of questions.

★ ★ ★

The girl Deirdre was waiting for me at the other side of the door. She smiled gently.

"You came just at the right time, Mr Faraday," she said. "Dad is really going to take a beating on this one."

"Not if I can help it," I said.

The girl glanced anxiously toward

160

the door of her father's office.

"He works too hard," she said. "Ever since mother died he's only had his work."

"And you," I reminded her. "I'd say he thinks a great deal of you."

The girl looked confused.

"Maybe," she said haltingly. "It takes a lot to know what dad's really thinking. Won't you take a seat?"

She indicated a bench set alongside a desk at the far side of the office. We would be out of earshot of the other girl here. She gave us a curious glance and then bent to her typing again.

"I'll give you my number and you can ring me when your father's ready to take this up again," I said.

I gave her the office and my home number. The Dacey girl jotted them down in a little red leather-bound book on the desk in front of her. Her glossy blonde hair was shining under the lamps and her blue eyes looked more appealing then ever behind the horn-rimmed spectacles. She looked up like she could read my thoughts. The cleaner ones anyway.

"You'd better have my home number as well," she said. "Just in case you want to contact me out of hours."

"That might be entirely possible, Miss Dacey," I said.

I glanced back over toward Tom Dacey's door.

"But don't you think it might be a little too close to home?"

The Dacey number grinned. She leaned forward at the desk and her eyes looked so clear and blue that I could almost see the sky in them.

"Father's broad-minded," she said.

I didn't answer that. The girl slid a large piece of pasteboard over. It had her phone number written on it in green ink in a firm, determined hand. Underneath she had written: Any Time. The words were underlined three times. I looked at her more closely as I put the card in my wallet. She had a pretty nice figure beneath the frilly white blouse. She put up her hand nervously and patted her already immaculate hair.

"What do you think's behind all this, Mr Faraday?"

"Your note or the plane crashes?" I said.

The girl sat back in the chair. Pink was flooding into her cheeks again. It looked quite becoming.

"The crashes of course, Mr Faraday."

There was a reproving tone in her voice which hadn't been there before.

"Could be Arab terrorists," I said. "But like I told your father, they seem to be pretty incompetent. There were no threats or demands and the explosions seem to have come entirely unexpectedly. That doesn't fit with the Arabs' track record."

The troubled expression was back on the girl's face now. She fiddled with the tip of a gold pencil on the blotter in front of her.

"You may be right, Mr Faraday."

"How does this tie in with the insurance?" I said.

"It makes it more complicated," the girl said. "The relatives of the passengers will be paid. But it's a long and elaborate process and sometimes takes years. Apart from that the policies are with many different companies. Dad and his partners act for everyone on a case like this though the companies usually send their own investigators to add weight."

"It seems one hell of a mess," I said.

The girl looked at me, her head on one side as though she meant to say something else. She apparently thought better of it because she closed her lips and got up as though the interview was closed.

"We're rather pressed today, Mr Faraday, as you can see," she said. "So if you'll forgive me . . ."

I got up too.

"Surely," I said. "You'll be in touch, then?"

The girl smiled.

"At the first possible moment," she said softly.

She turned and walked back across the office, toward the railing. I noticed then that beneath the short grey skirt she had really beautiful legs. A perfect matching set. A dry cough sounded at my elbow. I looked up to see an old man with grey eyes twinkling behind gold pince-nez.

"If you'll just get out of the way, young man," he said, "I'd like to get to my office."

The Dacey girl turned at the sound of his voice. She nodded brightly.

"Dad's having a rest just now, Mr Skidmore," she said. "He's been out all night."

Skidmore inclined his head.

"Terrible business," he said as though to himself. "I won't disturb him, Deirdre," he said.

I had my hand on the door when he spoke again. He looked from me to the Dacey number and then turned back.

"You could do worse, you know."

His dry chuckle followed me out the office and down the creaking staircase with the heavy balustrades. He might have had something at that.

13

IT was around five when I got back to the office. Stella met me when I was halfway through the waiting room door.

"How'd you make out?" she said brightly.

"Fixed up a working arrangement with the character who's investigating the aircraft explosion for the insurance companies," I said. I filled her in on the details.

Stella looked at me sharply.

"You have a smug expression," she said.

"Dacey has some nice help around the place," I said.

"I might have guessed," Stella said.

She put her hand on my arm before I got to the door of the inner office.

"We got a visitor," she said. "Nice little girl who wants your help."

"Quite a few of them do," I said. Stella gave me a pitying look.

"This is different, goof," she said. "Her uncle was one of those killed in the plane wreck."

I stopped and came back into the centre of the room with Stella so that we couldn't be heard from the inner office.

"What does she expect me to do?" I said. "This is an insurance job."

Stella shrugged.

"She wouldn't say. Said she'd rather wait for you. Her name's Janet Firestone."

"Sounds all right," I said.

"She is all right," Stella said. "But she's rather upset. I thought I'd warn you."

"Thanks," I said. "Heard anything more from Troon?"

"He phoned about an hour ago," Stella said. "He wondered if you could spare him some time tomorrow."

"I'll look by," I told her.

I went on in through the inner door.

The girl sitting with her legs crossed in the chair opposite my desk got up as we came in. She looked pretty nice. She had dark hair that was parted demurely in the middle. It was long and caught at the back by one of those buckle arrangements that women wear these days. She wore a well-tailored grey pyjama suit over a white silk shirt. Her face was brown and very lightly made up. She had a broad brow, very firm eyebrows. Her eyes were green. Right now they were a little red like she'd been crying.

She wore a very expensive-looking diamond ring on her right hand. Her height was about five feet ten, I should have said. Fairly tall for a girl of her build. I couldn't see much of it but what there was was nice. Her breasts strained forward beneath the lapels of the jacket. She looked to be around twenty-five.

"Mr Faraday?"

Her voice was low and well-modulated. She looked and sounded pretty 100-carat. She gave me a slim, well manicured hand to shake. I could feel the trembling of her body all the way down to her finger-tips. I asked her to sit down again and went around my own desk to sit opposite her. Stella closed the waiting room door and went over to the alcove. I heard the click of the percolator as she switched on.

"You read my thoughts," I said.

I smiled at the girl in front of me.

"You'd like a cup of coffee, Miss Firestone? You look as if you could do with one."

The girl leaned forward and bit her lip like she was having difficulty in keeping control of herself.

"That's very kind, Mr Faraday. It's about my uncle, John Firestone III."

"All in good time, Miss Firestone," I said. "Stella here brews the best cup of coffee in the world. We'll just wait a minute or two and then you can tell me all about it."

The girl gave me a tight little smile and dabbed daintily at the corner of her eye with a small lace handkerchief she took from a sling bag hung over the back of the chair. Stella came back into the room again. She gave me a big wink over the girl's shoulder as she reached her desk. The girl took a small gold plated cigarette lighter out of the bag.

"Do you mind?" she said hesitantly, opening a package of cigarettes.

"Do it all the time," I said.

I slid the big earthenware tray on my desk over in front of her and lit up myself. There was a nice blue plateau of smoke floating in the still air up by the ceiling when Stella put the cups down in front of us. It hid the cracks in the decor nicely. Stella went back to the alcove for her own cup. I figured she must walk about three miles a day brewing up. I grinned to myself. It certainly kept her fit. And it wasn't hard on her figure either.

I put my cigarette down on the edge of the tray and took the first few sips of coffee. The breeze in at the window was a little cooler now, the superheated air losing some of its bite.

"Your uncle was in the crash, I hear," I said. "I'm sorry."

The girl's shoulders shook.

"It was terrible, Mr Faraday, just terrible," she said.

She closed her fingers convulsively over the small square of handkerchief as though she meant to tear it into shreds.

"It looked pretty rugged," I said. "I saw it go down." The girl looked at me with a startled expression.

"You were there?"

I shook my head.

"I was about eight miles away. I just happened to see a ball of fire in the sky the other side of the city."

The Firestone girl nodded.

"All those people. It was just awful. I can hardly believe it. It would have been my uncle's sixty-fifth birthday next week."

"That's the way it goes, sometimes," I said. "It's tough, all right. But I'm

172

not quite clear as to how I can help you, Miss Firestone."

The girl shrugged.

"I'd like someone to represent my interests. I've shopped around a bit. I hear very good things of you in L.A."

"That's very kind, Miss Firestone," I said "But I still don't quite see . . . "

"More coffee, Miss Firestone?" Stella interrupted smoothly. She shot me a warning look as she reached over the girl's shoulder and picked up the beaker. Stella scooped my cup from the blotter.

"No need to ask you," she said.

"Too right," I told her.

I looked across to where Janet Firestone sat twisting her handkerchief between her two trembling hands.

"It's not that I'm unsympathetic, Miss Firestone," I said. "But I don't see what use I could be. You must have lawyers, insurance advisers; all these people would be able to help more than I could. I'd only get in the way."

"I'd be the best judge of that," the girl said. "You haven't heard my proposition yet."

I spread out my hands on the desk. "Take your time," I told her.

Stella was back again now, the aroma of freshly roasted beans in my nostrils. She smiled at the expression on my face. She went back to the alcove to fetch another cup for herself. Then she sat down at her own desk and stirred her coffee, saying nothing, with that marvellous tact of hers.

There was silence for a minute or two. I looked across at the window overlooking the boulevard. I sighed. I'd got a lot of threads on Troon's toys, two murders and now a plane crash. Apart from the fact that I didn't know what was happening I was doing great. The view outside the window was clouding over. The sunlight was fading. It looked like it might be setting in for rain again. I turned back to the girl.

"I take it your uncle was fairly well

174

fixed, Miss Firestone?"

The girl forced a tiny smile.

"Then you'll take the case, Mr Faraday?"

"We haven't got a case yet, Miss Firestone," I said. "But I'm willing to do what I can to help."

"That's more like it," Stella said.

She slid her scratchpad across toward her and picked up her gold pencil.

★ ★ ★

It was almost dusk now and the room was beginning to fill with smoke. Stella got up and switched on the fan. I put on my desk lamp. It made a vivid splash of yellow across the bottom of the Firestone girl's face, leaving her eyes in shadow. She looked mysterious and seductive that way. Stella sat with her chin cupped on her hands and watched me with very blue eyes. The light shimmered on the blonde bell of her hair so that it looked like burnished gold.

175

"Where was your uncle going?" I said.

The girl stubbed out her first cigarette and lit another.

"He had business in London," she said. "I told him not to go."

I sat back in my swivel chair and looked at her steadily.

"Care to enlarge on that?"

"He'd been warned not to," she said.

She rummaged around in her shoulder bag while Stella and I sat and waited. An oppressive atmosphere seemed to have settled over the office.

"This is why I wanted to retain your services," she said.

She came up with a folded square of brown paper and passed it over to me. Someone had scrawled two lines of a message on it in block lettering with a felt-nibbed pen. It said: IF YOU WANT TO LIVE DONT GO TO LONDON. ALF. I put the paper back on the desk where Stella could read it.

"Apart from the fact that he doesn't know where to put his apostrophes Alf doesn't seem a very literate gentleman," Stella said. "A Londoner presumably?"

"Come off it, Watson," I said. "You know very well the initials mean Arab Liberation Front."

Stella's eyes flashed.

"Just testing you," she said.

I turned back to the girl.

"When did this come?"

She shook her head.

"I don't know. My uncle showed it to me about two hours before he took off."

"Why should the Arabs care about your uncle one way or another?" I said. "Is he rich?"

The girl leaned forward in the chair. "Immensely, Mr Faraday. He's not a Jew but he has acute Zionist sympathies. He was going to London as part of a consortium which was arranging a multi-million dollar gift to the State of Israel."

There was a long silence. Stella

tapped with her pencil on very white teeth.

"That might explain a lot of things," I said. "But why didn't you take this to the police? You could get into a lot of trouble withholding evidence. And I could lose my licence for the same reason."

The girl put her handkerchief up to her mouth and I thought she was going to burst into tears.

"I'd rather retain you," she said. "I don't want the police in this."

"They're in already," I said. "And this is an important clue."

Stella got up and took the sheet of brown paper, put it in an envelope and then put the whole thing in the safe. The girl leaned forward so that all her face was in the glow of the lamp.

"A lot of people had an interest in seeing my uncle dead," she said fiercely. "That's why I want you in. And now that he's dead there's bound to be people squabbling over the estate."

"There's a man investigating this

smash," I said. "He's a big noise in insurance. I'm working with him. I'll have to turn this over to him. If you agree we'll stick by his decision. All right?"

The girl hesitated a moment.

"It's a deal, Mr Faraday," she said.

"If you'll forgive me for asking, Miss Firestone," I said. "Just where do you fit in all this?"

She smiled a hesitant smile.

"I don't inherit a penny," she said. "But I stand to collect a million dollars" worth of insurance. That's why I'd like your help."

She smiled again as she got up to leave.

"I'll be in touch," I said.

14

STELLA sat on the edge of her desk and looked at me critically. The girl had been gone fifteen minutes and neither of us had said anything yet.

"What do you think?" she said at last.

"I don't think anything," I said. "I passed that stage long ago. We got some plastic toys disappeared. We got one corpse under a truck. I know that wasn't an accident."

Stella didn't seem in a gabby mood so I went on.

"Then I get slugged as I find another corpse. The corpse disappears."

"When you come back the shop has a new owner," Stella said.

"Who acts guilty as hell," I told her.

I put my feet up on my old broadtop

and looked at the night sky outside the window. The neons were beginning to make a nice green, gold and mauve of the office decor.

"Mayer gets a bad case of St Vitus's Dance every time I start screwing at the neck of one of those ducks," I said.

"The ducks might or might not tie up with a bomb which wrecked a plane," Stella went on.

"Someone was watching me at the Fantastic Toyshop," I said. "Don't leave that out."

"I thought you had enough to be going on with," Stella said innocently.

"Now we got a nice little girl whose uncle gets a death-note before the fatal explosion," I said.

I got out my pack and lit a cigarette. I feathered smoke at the ceiling. Ideas were tossing around in my skull like billiard balls. Like billiard balls they only clicked tangentially and then went off somewhere else. It was a good way to go insane if you had nothing better to do.

"Apart from her wanting me to look after the million bucks she stands to collect when old Firestone kicked it," I said.

I took my feet down from the desk and focused up on Stella's knees through the smoke of my cigarette. It wasn't a difficult thing to do at any time. This time of the evening it was positively therapeutic. Stella saw the direction of my gaze and grinned. She didn't alter the position of her legs any though.

"I knew I should have taken up fretwork," I said. "It would have been a nice little living. A home hobbies shop down on Forty-Fourth Street. Strictly nine to five and you get to walk the dog on Sunday."

Stella snorted. Leastways the elegant noise she came out with was the nearest to a snort she would ever get.

"I've heard that before," she told the filing cabinet. "You'll feel better once you get a few ideas."

"I'll need more than ideas, honey,"

I said. "I could do with a good steak right now."

"Is that an invitation to dinner?" Stella said brightly.

"Not this time of the week," I said. "See if you can get hold of Dacey, will you? He'll probably be home by now."

Stella made a moué and picked up the phone. She dialled a number and then cupped the receiver in her hand.

"It sounds like a girl," she said.

I picked up the phone on my desk.

"I got news for you," I said. "It is a girl."

Stella put down her phone and started stacking the mail.

"I'm glad to hear from you, Mr Faraday," Deirdre Dacey said. "Dad was asking me to get hold of you."

"I'm the most get-holdable man you ever met," I said.

Stella coughed and moved round her desk.

"Would you like me to leave?" she said.

I grinned.

"Would it make any difference?"

Stella shook her head.

"Something important's come up," I said. "I have to see your father right away."

"No problem," the Dacey girl said. "He won't be home for an hour or two. He's still out at the Airport. But if you'd like to come on over for dinner . . . "

"It sounds great," I said.

"You got the address?" the girl said.

"I'm on my way," I told her.

Stella was already undoing the safe that we keep behind the large-scale map of L.A.

She handed me the note the Firestone number had left. It was now in a neat envelope with an identification number inked on it.

"I really should get a chit signed for it but Faraday Investigations is willing to waive protocol this time of night,"

Stella said. She glanced at her watch ostentatiously.

"You go on home, honey," I said. "And thanks for everything."

I switched off the desk lamp and waited for Stella to join me by the door.

"You sure you can handle it?" Stella said. "If you get hit on the head again we lose a vital piece of evidence."

"I think I can about manage for tonight," I said.

Stella put up her face and lightly kissed the lobe of my ear. I felt it right the way down to my socks.

"If you get topped again you know the way to my door," she said gently.

"I'd rather not try it again just yet," I said. "I'm still enjoying the effects of the last time around."

We rode down together to the ground floor. Then I picked up the Buick and started making time toward the Dacey girl's place.

★ ★ ★

185

Laurel Boulevard was up one of the canyons about an hour's drive across town. The Daceys lived in a big bungalow-style house set back behind well-shaved lawns. It was a fairly modest place for someone with Dacey's position. I tooled the Buick in over a red gravel drive and up to where two brass lanterns made twin pools of radiance in the gloom. There was a three-car garage at the side of the house and a sport-job of foreign make standing in front of the open doors. So I guessed they weren't too poor.

My Smith-Wesson .38 in its webbing harness made a reassuring pressure against my shoulder muscles as I eased out the Buick and started walking up the crazy concrete path that wound across the grass toward the front porch. Since my skull had been re-arranged at La Boutique Fantasque I'd decided to carry it on this case from here on in. The pain had gone now but I still felt a neuralgic twinge in my facial muscles from time to time.

The Dacey girl was coming through the door into the glassed-in entrance porch as I got to the steps. She ran down to meet me. Tonight she wore a white trouser suit that made a dazzling splash of incandescence in the gloom of the garden. She took both my hands in hers like we were two old friends.

"Glad you could come, Mike," she said in a low voice. "Minerva has cooked us something special. I hope you're hungry."

"Try me," I said.

I followed the girl up into the porch and through the main door of the house into the hall. This had black and white tiled paving and big bowls of tropical flowers set in front of mirrors which gave off a pungent aroma in the dusk. There was only one lamp burning in here; a wall sconce by one of the mirrors and the reflections gave back five different images of the girl.

I hadn't got time to admire them, though. A tall, busty woman with a coffee-coloured skin came through

187

from an arch under the stairway and chuckled throatily.

"We eat in fifteen minutes, Miss Deirdre," she called cheerily, giving me a critical look as she passed.

"If you want to wash up, there's a cloakroom at the foot of the stairs," the girl said.

When I rejoined her in the dining room five minutes later I saw the big mahogany table was already set for two. The girl was sitting at the head with me on her right and the light from the overhead chandelier cast a golden glow over her perfect skin. She'd done something different to her hair and its pale gold shimmered mistily in the light of the lamps. She'd left off her glasses too and her blue eyes looked candid and more immediate, with none of that far-away look the glasses gave her.

The room was a spacious one with woodblock floors and the furniture was heavy and discreet; it seemed to speak more of the late Mrs Dacey than the girl and her father. Though perhaps it was a little too early to tell. The girl looked at me with approval. She patted the chair at her side with a well-manicured hand.

"Minerva's going to serve as soon as we're ready," she said. "Do you want anything to drink beforehand?"

I shook my head and sat down at her right. The dark-skinned woman was back now with two silver bowls containing prawn cocktail and crushed ice. A chilled white wine slipped easily into tulip glasses as Minerva looked at us with a mischievous eye.

"Are you going to say something or shall I, Miss Deirdre?" she said.

The girl's face turned a pale pink.

"I'm sure I don't know what you mean," she said.

The dark woman gave an explosive gurgle of laughter.

"That's a bit different to what you said earlier tonight when you told me Mr Faraday was coming out here."

"Am I allowed to join in or is it closed-circuit?" I said.

The girl smiled, echoing Minerva's broad grin.

"It's just a joke between us, Mike. Pay no attention."

The dinner was one of the best I'd ever tasted. Not that I'm a connoisseur of food and wine. Too many half-digested meals at hamburger joints had blunted my taste buds. That and too many evenings spent in crummy joints where the atmosphere is composed of cigarette smoke and stale cooking smells in equal proportions. But at thirty-three I hadn't lost my appetite for the good stuff when I could get it. And this was good.

The girl said little, looking at me with shy smiles from time to time. She waited until the dark woman had gone out at the end of the meal. Then she picked up her cup and saucer.

"Guess we'll finish our coffee in the den, Mike. That will give Minerva a clear field."

"What does that give me?" I said.

I must have had one glass of wine

too many because I found my tongue slurring over the sentence. The girl looked at me with amusement. "You haven't seen the den yet," she said.

It was some place; pine panelled walls, with almost every inch of space covered with sporting prints or beasts that Dacey had slaughtered at one time or another. There was a big stone fireplace up at one end and a low fire of logs gave out an amber glow in the dusk. I went and stood up near the fireplace and looked at an antlered head that still seemed to express surprise.

"Fond of shooting, is he?" I said.

Deirdre Dacey grinned. She suddenly looked beautiful. She was sitting on a brown leather Chesterfield that would have taken six people with comfort and she looked bright and clear-minted in the white suit against the sombre background. I almost wished she'd kept the grey skirt on. She had sensational legs and I hadn't seen enough of them. She seemed to sense my thoughts because she looked at me enigmatically and subtly shifted her position.

I went and sat down next to her. I caught again a faint, elusive perfume that I couldn't quite place. I finished off my coffee and put it down on a small table at the end of the settee. "That was a great meal, honey," I said.

The girl moved over while I was doing that and handed me her own cup. She had to go in front of me to do so and I felt the soft warmth of her body against mine. A strand of her hair fell across my cheek. She put her face against mine and we sat like that for perhaps ten minutes, looking over toward the fire without saying anything. The house was quiet; there wasn't even the faint echo of Minerva moving about the kitchen. I wondered if that was what the dark woman had been smiling about earlier.

The girl's breath was doing things to the side of my face. I shifted position slightly, felt her mouth on mine. She was so hungry it felt like she'd never been kissed before. We surfaced after about ten minutes.

"I'm here on business, honey," I said.

"So am I," Deidre Dacey said.

She reached over and took one of my hands and put it gently on her firm breast. I let it stay there. After all, who was I to argue. But I still had some prudence though.

"What about Minerva?" I said.

The girl licked my ear with a pink tongue.

"She's gone out to a movie," she said.

I looked at the girl and smiled.

"Convenient," I said. "And what about your father?"

"I lied a little," the girl said calmly. "He won't be home for at least two hours."

I was still holding the girl and I pushed her gently away from me so that I could look at her properly. Her eyes were shining and she looked absurdly young in the dim light of the lamp at the end of the Chesterfield.

"Sure of yourself, weren't you?" I said.

The Dacey girl smiled a slow smile. She took my hand and put it in the open vee of her white jacket. I could feel the hurried rise of her breathing.

"Was I wrong?" she said.

I shook my head.

"Do you always make up your mind about people this quickly?"

"Not usually," the girl said calmly. "But you're something special."

"I'm just a beat-up private eye," I said. "Nothing special about me."

Deirdre Dacey came forward again and nipped the lobe of my ear with very white teeth.

"You let me be the judge of that," she breathed.

She reached over and caught the trailing flex of the table lamp. She extinguished the light. The gentle glow of the firelight made a crimson mask of her face.

She sat quite still as I undid her jacket, slid off the thin silk shirt underneath. She was already stepping out of the pants, sliding them down over thighs that seemed to go on for ever. There was a dark shadow between her legs as she kicked off her shoes and leaned toward me. I unhooked the half-cup bra she was wearing and her nipples jutted forward into the firelight.

When she was completely nude she lay back on the Chesterfield and let me examine her. Her eyes were half-closed and she had a lazy look on her face.

"Satisfied?" she said softly.

"Not yet," I said. "But I will be."

I was already unbuttoning my jacket. Deirdre's eyes widened as she took in my shoulder holster. She put out a pink-nailed hand and ran a finger down the butt of the Smith-Wesson.

"You won't need that tonight, Mike," she said.

I unbuckled the harness and put it on the carpet, kicked off my shoes. I knelt down between her legs. All the front of her body was open to me.

"We'll see, honey," I said. "I may need to give you a pistol whipping before we're through."

The girl giggled, squirmed into a more vulnerable position.

"You're a hard man, Mike."

I caught hold of her firmly, started to climb aboard.

"You can say that again," I said.

15

TOM DACEY'S big, crumpled face looked approvingly at me as he came through the door. Deirdre sat demurely at the end of the Chesterfield, her legs tucked beneath her, a book balanced on her lap. The fire had burned quite low now. I sat at the other end of the Chesterfield thinking back over the best hour I'd had in years. The girl was wearing a secret smile like that of the Mona Lisa.

Dacey put his briefcase down on a table near the fire-place and sagged into a leather easy chair. He looked from me to the girl and then back again. Glints of humour were dancing in his faded blue eyes.

"Been here long?" he said in a mild voice.

"Hours and hours," the girl said

calmly. "We had dinner. We got quite tired of waiting for you."

"I had to go down to the Airport again," Dacey said.

He turned to me.

"Got some close-up pictures here that would interest you, Mike."

Dacey had put another smaller briefcase on the floor by his chair. Now he picked it up and sifted about in its contents. I went over to stand by him while he rummaged.

"I could do with a whisky, Deirdre," he said.

The girl got up and went over to a pine sideboard and busied herself with glasses. Dacey stopped his probing about and looked at her affectionately.

"Don't know what you two found to do," he said jovially. "It must have been a boring evening, Mike."

"I wouldn't say that," I said.

I looked at the girl as she came back with Dacey's drink. Her ears were a bright pink and she avoided my eyes. I shook my head as she held out a glass.

"I think I've had enough for one evening, thanks.

"Nonsense," Dacey said. "At least have some coffee before you go. Deirdre won't mind."

The girl gave me a secret look as she went out the door. It was so strong it started boring holes in my socks. Dacey smacked his lips over his drink and then put the glass down on the broad edge of his leather chair.

"I must be getting old, Mike," he said. "It was in front all the time."

He got out a strong brown envelope backed with card. I took it over to the Chesterfield and sat down. It was then I noticed the frilly edge of lace jammed down against one of the side cushions. The girl had been in such a hurry to take her things off she must have over-looked it. I wondered if Dacey had spotted it. His bright blue eyes were fixed on me unwinkingly. I couldn't see any guile in them.

I put the envelope across my knees and undid it. There was a big sheaf

199

of glossies inside. I spread them out. Dacey took another swig at his drink and turned his eyes toward the embers of the fire. I hooked the scrap of lace and nylon out from the side cushion and eased it into my right hand trouser pocket.

The pictures showed scraps of material that looked as if they'd been blasted and scorched; there was a legend along the base of each picture and a scale in inches. The close-ups of the fragments were of a type familiar to me over many years.

"The lab boys did a good job," I said.

Dacey grunted.

"About as good as could be expected," he said. "It isn't easy."

He turned back to me and stuck out a stubby forefinger.

"Look at numbers one and six," he said.

I turned to the prints he'd indicated. The stills appeared to be of a trade-mark. It was something I'd seen before.

There was just a trace of black lettering on the scorched plastic. One piece of debris had a fairly clear M and something that looked like part of an A. The other contained a cipher that looked like a faded C.

"Looks like the trade-mark of the Maroc Trading Company," I said. "Should be easy to find out if we compare it with an original."

"That's what I hoped you'd say," Dacey said.

He looked up as the girl came in again with a tray and coffee cups. She dragged a small oak table over from one side of the room and put it down midway between the Chesterfield and the easy chair.

"Make it black, honey," Dacey said.

He turned back to me.

"The lab boys said the explosive had been packed inside a child's plastic toy. They figured it was something like a duck."

"They were dead right," I said. "It's one of Troon's most popular lines."

Dacey took his coffee cup from the girl and his eyes had no tiredness in them.

"Guess we'll go see Mr Troon tomorrow," he said. "I heard you came up with something."

"An added complication," I said.

I took the cup the girl handed me, trying to forget hair like silk which brushed against my face as she bent over me, and the warm, clean perfume of her body. I told Dacey about Janet Firestone's visit. He sat and watched me with expressionless eyes. The girl had gone to sit at the other end of the Chesterfield.

She kept her eyes on me and said nothing. Dacey shifted almost imperceptibly in his chair as I told him about the warning message to the old man. I got up and took the envelope out my jacket pocket. I passed him the sheet. There was a long silence in the room as he studied it: he let his breath out in a brief, expressive explosion of sound.

"Jesus Christ, Mike," he said. "We got a hot potato here. The lab boys ought to have this right away. Why in hell's name didn't the girl contact the police direct?"

"We been through all that," I said. "She had her reasons. And she's my client. I told her I was putting you in the picture. But I'm not authorized to go any farther."

Dacey gave me a withering look.

"We'll both be going up the river if we hang on to this too long," he said. "This is Grade A evidence."

"Why don't you just have your lab people run over it for a report," I said. "Confidential, of course. Then we see what we come up with. That way we don't waste any time."

Dacey's eyes were twinkling.

"And bring the police in afterwards. Why not? We can go up the river together."

"You said that before," I told him.

Dacey grinned. He rubbed his chin with one big hand again.

203

"We got a hell of a lot to sort out here," he said. "Any ideas?"

"We ought to have a talk with Troon in the morning," I said. "We can take it on from there."

"All right."

Dacey stood up.

"I'm going to hit the sack. I'm bushed. And there's no use worrying any more about this tonight." He gave me a heavy wink.

Deirdre Dacey turned pink. She bent her head down into her coffee cup.

"Better ring Deirdre in the morning and let me know the arrangements," Dacey said. "I'll leave things free so that we can meet up to suit all parties."

"Right," I said.

"Night, honey," Dacey said.

The girl got up to kiss him and then went over to stand by the fire. Dacey marched over to the door and disappeared without turning his head. I guess he had a lot on his mind at the moment. I went over to stand by the girl as she stood looking down into the embers of the fire.

"It's been quite an evening," I said.

"You can say that again," the girl breathed.

She put her arms round my neck and we kissed. We seemed to stay like that for an hour. Then a door slammed. The girl gently pushed me away.

"Enough for one night," she said. "We can take this up some other time."

I heard heavy footsteps in the hall. Minerva came into the doorway of the den and stood looking at us with bright, malicious eyes.

"Good movie?" I said.

The housekeeper's face broke up in a brilliant smile. I noticed she had very even, perfect teeth against the smooth creaminess of her face.

"Not as good as yours," she said cheerfully.

"We had a real double feature," Deirdre Dacey said calmly. She flashed a quick, warm smile at me.

"Well, I'll be off to bed then,"

Minerva said, turning around in the doorway like she'd lost her sense of direction.

"Don't forget to lock up when this gentleman goes."

We stood and waited until the echo of her footsteps had died away on the staircase.

The girl came with me to the door. We kissed again. When we'd finished I put the scrap of nylon and lace into her hand.

"You forgot your handkerchief," I said.

The girl's face turned a warm scarlet beneath her tan under the dim light of the hall lamp.

"Christ, Mike," she said. "I hope dad didn't see."

"It was on the divan," I said. "I got to it in time."

The girl twisted up her face like she was going to cry.

"Don't stand too long in the night wind," I said. "You must feel the draught."

The girl thumped me with her closed fist on the side of my jaw.

"Bastard," she said affectionately.

I looked back as I got down the steps and saw her slim silhouette still immobile in the porch. I reversed the Buick out and drove home to Park West to hit the sack.

★ ★ ★

Albert Troon's eyes looked frosty. He sat in back of his desk with Myriam Van Cleef in a swivel chair at his side and glanced unhappily from me to Tom Dacey and then back again.

"If what you tell me is correct, Mr Faraday," he said, "I'm to infer that you suspect either myself or Miss Van Cleef leaked information deliberately to the factory?"

I shook my head.

"There's no need to get het-up, Mr Troon. But somebody at the factory knew I was coming all right. I was set up and topped by people who knew

207

what they were doing. Fortunately I came around in time to get out before the law arrived."

Troon shifted in his chair and blinked at the girl.

"Whatever way you slice it, we got a lot of trouble," he said. "Of course you realize, Mr Dacey, that anybody could have bought these ducks over the counter of any toy store. We sell hundreds of thousands of them every year."

Dacey didn't seem to hear what Troon had said. He sat in one of Troon's chairs and kept his tired blue eyes on Myriam Van Cleef's face.

"Except that we figure the stuff used for the blast was packed into one of the toys stolen from your factory," I said. "That way there's no traceback."

"I don't get it," Troon said helplessly.

"We're dealing with very clever people, Mr Troon," Dacey said. "Anybody who bought these sort of toys across the counter would have a face and recognisable characteristics.

Which make him traceable. Which makes the risk too high if you're blowing up airliners."

Troon blinked again. He wore a mauve bow tie today that floated like some fierce tropical butterfly beneath his lean features. He scratched his mosslike sandy hair like everything was too much for him and looked helplessly at the Van Cleef girl.

"You realize everything we've told you today must be kept absolutely between these four walls," Dacey said.

Troon licked his lips.

"No worry about us," he said. "Just what do you intend to do?"

Dacey looked at me quickly.

"I think we'll be keeping that to ourselves for the moment, Mr Troon," he said.

Troon flushed.

"Don't forget you're still working for me, Mr Faraday," he said.

"I haven't forgotten," I told him. "But we've got other considerations with the airliner blast. I'm tagging along behind Mr Dacey here."

Troon nodded.

"Fair enough," he said. "Just so long as you keep me posted. This is getting to be quite a nightmare."

"It wasn't much fun for the people in the plane," Dacey said mildly.

Troon flushed again. He shifted awkwardly in his chair.

"I didn't mean that," he said. "If I've inadvertently . . ."

"Forget it," Dacey said, rising to his feet. "We'll be drifting now. Keep you posted."

Troon got up and shook hands with us both. For the first time he looked really absent-minded and helpless. Myriam Van Cleef got up with a sinuous movement of her body.

"I'll show you out," she said.

She went over and held the door for Dacey. I went through and waited for her to catch me up. The Van Cleef number treated me to another stretch of her beautiful teeth. Her blonde hair shone under the light of the chromed overhead lamps. Dacey waited near the railed-off enclosure and looked at me wistfully.

"How you making out?" I said, jerking my head toward the door of Troon's office. A plastic giraffe's head looked at me glazedly from over Myriam Van Cleef's shoulder.

"In what way?" the girl said.

"Personally," I said.

She grinned.

"He took me out to dinner last night."

"Nice going," I said.

The girl looked curiously over toward Tom Dacey's big figure.

"You can't say much about this business?"

I shook my head.

"I'm working with the insurance boys now. I got a few ideas of my own. But I'd rather say nothing until I'm sure. But I don't think there's anything for Troon to worry about."

The girl hesitated.

"It's turning out pretty nasty," she said.

"It always does," I said. "Every time anyone calls me in and I start stirring things up."

The girl nodded.

"I know what you mean. I'd be grateful if you'd keep me posted."

"You'll be the first to know," I told her.

We shook hands and I rejoined Dacey. We walked down the stairs together. He looked thoughtful.

"Nice girl, that."

"I guess so," I said. "She's making a play for Troon but he's too dumb to see it."

Dacey shot me a shrewd glance.

"Well, well," he said. "That's what too much contact with toys does for you."

He looked wistfully back down the corridor.

"I wouldn't mind taking a whirl there myself."

He shook his head.

"Troon's too tied up with his business. Did you get those giraffes? And that walking penguin? There's a retarded childhood in there somewhere."

I grinned.

"If the Van Cleef girl gets hold of him he'll grow up in a hurry," I said. "I wouldn't worry about him."

"He's your client," Dacey said.

We were at the bottom of the staircase by now. The big man reached in his inner pocket and brought out the envelope with the message I'd given him last night.

"The lab people went over it," he said. "Nothing useful. The paper was made here in L.A. It's used for wrapping by millions of people over the States. Ordinary felt-nibbed pen used. Buy them in any corner store."

"No prints?" I said.

Dacey shook his head.

"Whoever wrote the note used gloves. That mean anything to you?"

"Sure," I said. "We're up against some cunning bastards. The more I look at it the less it looks like Arabs."

Dacey rubbed his chin.

"You and me both."

He stopped in the middle of the vestibule and looked at me searchingly for a moment.

"I'm not used to working with characters like you, Mike. There's something on your mind."

"We've got a lot of facts and no case at the moment," I said. "My bet is the factory end. I'll be starting there."

Dacey rubbed his chin again.

"I'd like to know your plans in case anything happens."

"Sure," I said "I always believe in insurance myself."

16

NUMBER 4466 Ventura Drive was a long bungalow in the Spanish style set back behind a low hedge of evergreens, now wilting in the heat.

It was dusk when I got there and I parked the Buick in a layby about two hundred yards down and smoked a cigarette while I waited for the light to die from the sky. The traffic went by on the main stem a quarter of a mile away, white-wall tyres shirring in the tropical evening. Street lamps cast pools of light and far out across the Pacific a jet-trail made a silvery scar on the afterglow.

I got out the Buick and closed the door quietly behind me. The Smith-Wesson made a light pressure against my shoulder as I crossed the sidewalk and got up on to the shaven turf of the surround. I walked back down to the place I wanted and went up a cement path that wound between flower-beds. The house was dark and shuttered and had that look houses have when people have gone a long way off.

But I didn't let that fool me. Dacey and I were messing in a business which had some nasty characters behind it and I had to get in fast. One of the ends was here and something had to break soon. It wouldn't do any good calling at the toyshop. I guessed I'd find it closed anyway. I was up to the porch now and I circled around on the grass, getting my bearings.

I went down another path that led past a two-car garage. There was a light-coloured convertible in the garage. I held my hand over the engine-grille. It was still warm. I bent down below the windows as I went in rear of the house. There was a second area of grass here and I could see the netting of a tennis court silhouetted against the dying light of the sky.

I went across the grass, my size nines making no sound, keeping close in to the wall. I went up on to the kitchen door. I tried the brass handle. It turned noiselessly on well-oiled tumblers. I had the Smith-Wesson out now, holding it at my side. I opened the door quickly and slid through the gap, closing it behind me, my fingers round the door edge to prevent it slamming.

There was no-one in the kitchen. It was a big place, running half the length of the house. There was enough light in here to see it had pine-panelled walls and solid Scandinavian furniture. There were steel-sinks and draining boards set along the side with the windows, an antique pine dresser and big cupboards screwed to the wall.

I waited until my eyes adjusted to the light. The faint ticking of a clock came from somewhere outside the half-open kitchen door at the end. That and the monotonous dripping of a tap in the sink were the only sounds in here. The tap got on my nerves but I didn't want to turn it off at this point. That didn't suit my purposes.

I could see better now. I went on down the kitchen, moving slowly on the tiles, testing each step, making sure I was was well back from the dark edge of shadow at the far door. If there were someone in the hallway I didn't want to be against the light from the windows. I stopped halfway down. The ticking of the clock was louder now and the dripping of the tap went on. It made a mournful sound that fretted at the edges of the silence.

There was a large, family size Frigidaire up this end, beyond the last of the sink drainers. The low hum of a refrigeration unit cut through the ticking of the clock. A big freezer chest was set between the Frigidaire and the far wall. I stood there for perhaps a minute, listening to the clock, the dripping tap and the pumping of my own heart.

I moved over toward the door as a board creaked somewhere. A muscle fretted in my cheek. I lifted the Smith-Wesson and waited. There was a faint shadow crawling at the corner of my eye. I moved my head, focused up. A dark triangle of something was hovering against the white background of the freezer chest. I went over toward it. A piece of cloth was sticking out from under the lid. It looked like the material of a man's suit.

I felt the old familiar scratching at the base of my spine. I kept the barrel of the Smith-Wesson high as I stepped forward. I lifted the lid of the freezer chest with my left hand. It came up easily, a fluorescent tube in the lid snapping on at the same moment.

The interior was a mass of frosting. The light sparkled on the rime thickly caking something that was lying on top of the ordinary contents. Ice was dusted like flour over the suit and shirt. A thin film of ice covered the stubbled beard and made the wide, staring eyes glisten even more brilliantly.

I lowered the gun and put the lid of

the chest back against the tiling. For the second time within three days I was gazing down at the corpse of the man I'd last seen in the office at La Boutique Fantasque. I turned as a boot squeaked on the parquet and a darker shadow came flailing at me from the dusky oblong of the door.

* * *

I got the gun up and heard a gasp as I raked it across a chest like a barrel. The big man grunted as I used my knee and then we were somersaulting across the kitchen together. I'd been prepared for him so I wasn't off guard. I broke away and got my instep behind his leg. I heard a crash as he went skidding farther down the tiling. I got to the light switch while he was completing his session from Les Patineurs.

The ox-like character in the natty grey suit groaned as his cropped head came in contact with the base of one of the sink units. His heels had made a nice scuffing mark across the floor. He blinked his eyes and tears of pain ran down to the corners of his mouth. I went and locked the door to the hallway and then got a chair and came back while he was doing that. I put one foot up on the chair and rested my gun-hand on my knee.

I looked from the man in the grey suit to the corpse in the freezer and then back again while the former fought for breath. He struggled up in the end and rested his back against a cupboard door.

"You got no right in here," he panted.

"You got a point," I said. "Just keep talking."

The big man scowled. He had a white, pasty face and the heavy bones underneath gave it a lumpy look. Right now a trickle of blood from his right temple down his cheek wasn't improving his appearance. He had a tight gash of a mouth and very square teeth like you sometimes see in boxers. His eyes were as black as his expression.

"I know you?" he said.

"You ought to," I said. "Name's Faraday. I was out at the Maroc Trading Company just the other day."

The big man shrugged. He was breathing more easily now and he put up one big hand and wiped the blood off his cheek.

"That supposed to mean something?"

"You tell me," I said. "Maroc's got a manager out there who's a little too gabby. He told the overseer I was coming out to poke around. You're the overseer. See what I'm driving at."

The big man scowled again. He tried to get up. I waved the Smith-Wesson at him.

"I'd prefer you down there," I said.

"I ought to call the police," he grumbled.

"Be my guest," I said. "They'd be really interested in the corpse in the freezer."

The big man shot a wild glance over

at the corner of the kitchen like he hadn't noticed the open ice-chest. He licked his lips.

"What do you want here?" he said sullenly.

"Answers," I said. "And I'm going to get them. Like what Alex Kinross, the shop proprietor over there is doing dead in your freezer. Or why you or one of your chums topped me when I found the body. Those will do for starters. I'll think of some others presently."

Reynolds reached in his inside jacket pocket. I lined the Smith-Wesson up on his gut while he did that. He carefully eased out a crumpled package of cigarettes and lit up. He ground the spent match into the tiling at his side and put the package down carefully next him. He leaned back against the cupboard door and closed his eyes like he was thinking up his story.

"Supposing we made a deal?" he said, his eyes still closed.

I shook my head.

"No deal," I said. "Just answers."

"It's your move then," he said.

His breathing was less agitated now and he seemed to be regaining his composure. The blood on his cheek was drying.

I lifted the Smith-Wesson and held it steadily until the sight was aligned on his right eyeball. He tried to face it out but after about three seconds he flinched away.

"Don't make me lose my temper," I said.

Reynolds shook his head.

"No go," he said. "I been worked over by better characters than you."

"I'll spell it out for you," I said. "Then we'll compare notes."

I reached out my hand and Reynolds put his pack in it. It was the same brand I smoked. I lit up and feathered smoke at the kitchen ceiling. I watched him carefully all the time but he didn't make any moves. He looked too beat up for the moment.

"I don't know what's behind all

this yet but I got some ideas," I said. "Some parties wanted to commit sabotage on a big scale. They hit on the idea of fixing up the explosive inside kids' plastic toys. They needed a lot of toys because they had to make experiments. So they chose Troon's factory. There was an ex-con named Curtis who was one of the truckies there. They got him to lose a load from time to time."

Reynolds gave a snorting noise. He had his eyes down toward the floor but I could see the fingers holding the cigarette trembling a little.

"Big-time larceny," he said.

"That wasn't the point," I told him. "If they'd bought the stuff over the counter someone might have identified them. This way was easier. It worked fine until Curtis started shipping loads off his own bat. He was making a little money on the side."

I took the cigarette out of my mouth. My throat was getting dry with all this talking.

"What's the point of it all?" Reynolds said.

"I'm coming to that," I said.

"Curtis was well paid for his loads but he started in business for himself. Then the management noticed the losses. Troon called me in. I went out there and you put the finger on me."

Reynolds swore. He started to get up. I took my foot down from the chair and hit him lightly across the side of the head with the barrel of the Smith-Wesson. He yelped with pain and crashed back against the cupboard doors. His face wrinkled and tears started oozing out his eyes. Another thin trickle of blood started down his face to join the first. I put my foot back on the chair again and steadied up the Smith-Wesson.

"I told you to take it easy," I said.

Reynolds looked at me with smouldering eyes. He reached out with a shaky hand and picked up his cigarette, which had fallen to the floor.

"Don't let me catch you on the

sidewalk one of these dark evenings," he said between clenched teeth.

"Not much fear of that where you're going," I said.

"Why me?" Reynolds said sullenly.

"It had to be you," I said. "It couldn't have been anyone else. Maltz has been a highly entrusted employee of Troon's for many years. I ruled him out. But he's got a loose tongue. He admitted he'd told you about my visit to the plant. So that let you in."

Reynolds shifted up against the cupboards. Tears were still trickling down his cheeks.

"Why would I finger you?" he said.

"That's for you to say," I told him. "But because you passed the message on Curtis got killed. Whoever rubbed Curtis killed Kinross the same evening. And arranged for me to be topped and left with a break-in rap hanging over me."

I glanced over toward the freezer to where Kinross's frosted features stared glassily up to the ceiling.

"You're going to have a hell of a job to prove all this," Reynolds gritted. He tried a jaunty puff at his cigarette but he was still trembling so much he didn't quite make it.

"Maybe," I said. "But things are beginning to add up. Whoever killed Curtis and Kinross couldn't afford to let me get too close. It had to be pretty important. And it meant they'd pretty well finished the operation."

"How'd you figure that?" Reynolds said.

"Kinross," I said. "He was the expert. They needed someone to make the bomb mechanism. Tricky stuff, that. Kinross was a direct lead. And I was on my way to La Boutique Fantasque."

I looked down at Reynolds sprawled at my feet and waved the Smith-Wesson at him.

"I'm getting a lot of the ends but I still need the people behind the operation. If you want to draw a light sentence I expect to get the rest from you."

The big man twisted his mouth into a smile.

"You expect a lot, gumshoe."

"I've always been optimistic," I said. "Besides, as far as they're concerned you're expendable."

I levelled up the Smith-Wesson on his face again. Sweat started to bead his forehead.

"So far as I'm concerned too," I said. "Characters who blow innocent people to glory find me a little short on sympathy."

Reynolds licked his lips.

"Christ, I had nothing to do with that . . . " he started to say.

"Save it," I told him. "You're wasting breath. The man at the boutique. A character called Mayer. He's got to be in on it. He'll have flown by now. I want to find him. And a lady who leaves perfume floating around. There's bound to be a lady in there somewhere."

I pulled back the hammer of the Smith-Wesson.

"I'm not too particular how I find out," I said. "Two people have been rubbed already. A third won't make much difference."

Reynolds had a desperate glint to his eye. His left hand stabbed convulsively at the kitchen floor.

"You wouldn't dare," he said.

"Try me," I told him.

The explosion of the gun seemed to hammer at the ear-drums in the low-ceilinged kitchen. A big hole was blown in the front of the cupboard about a foot from Reynolds' head. Splinters rained about the floor and I could hear the bullet ricochet from the brick wall somewhere behind the cupboard and rattle about among the metal pans. My ear-drums were singing and Reynolds' face looked white and crucified through the thick blue smoke that hung in the air. He looked at me incredulously. His throat was so dry he could hardly speak.

"You must be mad," he whispered huskily when he found his voice.

He couldn't stop his lower lip from trembling.

"Just angry," I said. "And in a hurry. The next one will be right between your eyes."

I lifted the gun again. Reynolds was already down flat on the floor, his hands over his head. His shoulders were shaking.

"Don't do it," he whispered. "The woman you want is called Carol Twining."

"Where will I find her?"

"Cortina Apartments," he said. "No. 201."

"What's your part in this?" I said.

"I used to work for her," Reynolds said. "When she knew I had a job at the Maroc factory she sent for me. She said she wanted toy samples without anybody knowing. She paid me well."

Reynolds shifted up. He turned a white, sick face toward me.

"Honest to Christ, I thought it was just some rival toy firm chipping in.

I didn't know anything about Arabs blowing up aircraft, only what I read in the papers."

"There was nothing about that in the papers," I said. "You knew all right."

Reynolds licked his lips again. He shook his head.

"Not until a couple of days ago. I got a phone call. I was warned I was in too deep to back out."

"That was to keep your mouth shut," I said. "It's too late now."

I took my foot off the chair and tapped Reynolds behind the ear with the pistol barrel while he was still trying to explain. He went out in mid-sentence. I checked he was still breathing all right. I went out to the garage.

There was no-one around and the rest of the house was empty. I had to move fast if I wanted to crack the case before the law moved in. I found some cord and bound Reynolds securely.

Then I got the hell out, found a pay-booth, phoned Stella and told her to contact Dacey over Reynolds. I got back in the Buick and drove across town.

THE Cortina Apartments was a big block which had a corner restaurant, plenty of grass in front and an air of chrome and plush opulence. It was around seven-thirty when I got there and cocktail time judging by the people in the bar. I drove the Buick in through a wrought iron gateway and parked it in rear of a Lincoln convertible and as far away from the Mercedes and Bentleys as possible. It was a bit too rich for my financial blood and I didn't want to be conspicuous this evening.

I was crossing the lobby when I spotted a familiar figure among the people just going in through the bar entrance. I say figure advisedly. It was undulating in all the right places. The girl turned round as I touched her lightly on the shoulder. She looked surprised. She disengaged herself from a group just going in the bar and turned back to me.

"I didn't expect to see you here, Mr Faraday," Janet Firestone said.

"Nor I you," I said. "Sorry to break up the party but I wanted to have a word with you anyway."

"I sometimes drop in of an evening," the girl said. "To have a quick drink with friends. Nothing important. Let's find a table."

I held the door for her and we went on in. The place was got up in Alpine style with stone walls and lots of cedar panelling. There was a massive fireplace up near the bar and alpenstocks and crossed skis hanging on the wall. It was all right if you liked that sort of thing.

A captain of waiters in a white jacket glided up like his feet were on castors and took our order. The girl asked for a cocktail; I stuck to beer. It was dim in here and we had a corner booth so that I could keep my eye on the whole area. It was a little awkward meeting the Firestone number because I was in a hurry to see Carol Twining. If Reynolds got free and phoned her before I got to the apartment it would blow things badly.

She waited until the drinks were on the table before she spoke again. The Firestone girl looked a little more controlled than when we'd met in my office. She still wore her dark hair parted in the middle and her green eyes were rested and sparkling with humour now. Her teeth looked very white against the even tan of her face. Tonight she wore a white sweater with a gold clasp on the right breast. The sweater was buckled in over her flat belly with a black leather belt.

She wore dark blue tailored trousers that undulated every time she moved. They looked like they'd been sprayed on to her buttocks. Altogether she was a pretty high-powered number.

"Have you any news?" she said over

the rim of her glass.

She fumbled in a small black leather shoulder bag and found a wisp of handkerchief.

"Things have been happening," I said. "I might be in a position to tell you something by tomorrow."

Janet Firestone raised her eyebrows.

"You sound as though you're on to something. Anything that will solve this horrible mystery about the crash. When I think of my uncle . . . "

She broke off and made a convulsive movement of her hands on the top of the table.

"It doesn't do any good," I said. "I'll tell you just as soon as there's anything to tell."

The girl sipped at her glass moodily.

"Strange we should meet like this. You have business in the building?"

"Sort of . . . " I said. "Incidentally, I've seen Dacey. The insurance man I was telling you about. He's playing ball."

The girl nodded. Her lips parted in

a faint smile as she looked at me approvingly.

"Did you find out anything about the warning message sent to my uncle?"

"We've had it gone over by the lab," I said. "Nothing helpful though. Ordinary felt nib pen. Paper made here in L.A. but could have been bought anywhere."

I got out my pack of cigarettes and offered one to the girl. She shook her head.

"I don't normally. Not unless I'm under stress."

I lit up and put the spent match stalk in the glass bowl in the middle of the table. The bar was filling up now and the level of the chatter was rising.

"Something I didn't quite understand," I said. "I believe your uncle was on his way to England when the plane crashed. It was my impression it was coming in to land."

The girl shook her head.

"The pilot had turned back for some

reason. Perhaps they found something wrong. Didn't Mr Dacey tell you that?"

I shrugged.

"We never got around to discussing it, that's all. We've had a lot of ground to cover."

The girl smiled again.

"Sure," she said. "Sorry if I sounded a little abrupt. But this whole business has me on edge."

"Understandable, Miss Firestone," I said.

I finished my drink and got up.

"I don't want to keep you from your friends. And I do have an appointment."

"Surely." The girl got up too.

She held out a small, warm hand hesitantly.

"You know where to reach me if anything breaks. Anything at all. We haven't discussed your fee yet."

I shook my head.

"Time enough to discuss that when I've done something for you."

The girl smiled. "As you wish,

Mr Faraday. You're very scrupu-
lous . . ."

She hesitated, looked almost embarrassed for a moment.

"For a private eye, you were going
to say," I told her. "I still have some
scruples, yes. One of them relates to
taking money for services rendered.
The police will have to know about
that note pretty soon. You'll need my
help then."

I paused and looked around the
room. The place was filling up rapidly.
I was looking at a man in the end booth
of a row of phone kiosks. He looked
vaguely familiar.

"Why I haven't got around to going
into your case in detail is because I'm
still tied up on the same business,"
I said.

The girl lifted her drink from the
table and finished it before setting it
down again.

"I understand, Mr Faraday. I'm at
your disposal whenever you want to see
me. Your secretary has my address."

"How about tomorrow?" I said.

"That would be fine," the Firestone number said. "You have only to ring. I'll be home all day."

"Until tomorrow then," I said.

I left her standing there by the table and went on out.

★ ★ ★

I crossed the marble-floored lobby and waited with a group of people in front of the mahogany elevator cage. There was a pretty leisurely atmosphere in here. I could smell money from the hushed tones of the gold-braided staff to the whiff of cigars and perfume. All the stuff that went with real crocodile-skin shoes and handbags.

The cage came down eventually and I got in. I wanted the fourth floor and I had to wait until three matrons with poodles, an elderly man with a face like a retired Colonel, and an obvious fairy with marcelled hair and tinted glasses had got out first. We stopped at every floor and more people were getting on all the time. It was that sort of place.

Apartment No. 201 was at the end of a long corridor that looked like something out of an Antonioni movie: black glass walls that stretched away to infinity; concealed lighting; evergreen plants; Mexican pottery jars; and a thick white carpet underfoot that gave back a pallid sheen from the black walls. I began to feel like Franz Kafka in one of his depressed moods before I'd gone halfway down it.

No. 201 had a polished oak door with a spy-hole and lots of expensive brass fittings glistening all over it. There was a voice-box set alongside the door and a brass frame into which a card bearing the name of the occupant of the apartment would normally rest. It was empty though. I frowned at it for a moment or two before I hit the door-bell. There was a faint jangling from far away, only half-heard over the hum of the air conditioning.

The door was opened quite suddenly

and I found myself looking at a familiar face. The big man smiled rather weakly and stepped back. I followed him into the hall of the apartment.

"I've been expecting you, Mr Faraday," he said.

"It's unlikely to say the least," I said. "I didn't know I was coming myself until an hour ago."

The big man shook his head.

"Just hold still," he said.

It was only then I saw the unmistakable bulge in the right-hand pocket of his jacket.

"Even I can't help blowing a hole in you at this range," he said.

The door slammed suddenly behind me. Before I could move a shadow crawled at the corner of my eye and I felt a sharp pricking sensation on my left wrist: my hand was halfway to the Smith-Wesson holster before the floor came up to meet my face and all the colours of my surroundings bleached out into darkness.

18

THERE was a humming noise and vibrations in my head. A light bulb flickered, receded and then steadied up in focus. I was lying on my back looking at a metal ceiling. I retched and waves of nausea swept over me. A sponge was passed across my forehead and water ran down my face.

"Feeling better, Mr Faraday?" a woman's soothing voice said.

"Like hell I am," I said.

Leastways that was what I meant to say. It came out as a croaking noise with no meaning. I closed my eyes and tried to fight the nausea. Full consciousness came back. The last thing I remembered was Mayer's smile as I went out. I could hear normally now. The humming roar wasn't just noises in my head. I opened my eyes again; metal bolts in the ceiling were vibrating. The face of a middle-aged woman was poised over mine. She looked kindly and concerned. She had some sort of nurse's outfit on.

"Where the hell am I?" I said.

"On your way to San Francisco, Mr Faraday," the woman said soothingly. "We're just turning over the sea."

I struggled up. I felt as weak as a cat but the woman couldn't push me down. She looked even more concerned.

"I hope there's not going to be any trouble, Mr Faraday. I was told you wouldn't be a troublesome patient."

"What the devil are you yacking about, woman?" I said.

The nurse licked her lips and moved away from the metal cot on which I was lying. I felt stronger by the second. Sunlight was stabbing in through a small, metal-framed window. I could see the sea sparkling below as the aircraft went into a steady turn.

"Let's have it," I said. "I'm no more a patient than you are."

I got my legs over the side of the cot. I was wearing some sort of white smock which reached to my ankles like a night-gown. Any other time I would have laughed. But I was treating this deadly seriously. I could see now we were in a small metal compartment, probably at the rear of the aircraft. There was some luggage stacked up at one end.

The woman had retreated to the bulkhead. Her eyes expressed alarm and she shot a glance once or twice at the metal door about six feet from where she was standing. I closed my eyes again as the plane rocked slightly. When I opened them I could recognise Santa Monica Bay with the beaches of Venice just sliding past on the starboard side.

"How long have we been airborne?" I said.

"Just this minute," the nurse said.

I slid off the cot and went over toward her. I wasn't dizzy any more and I could feel the strength coming back every second. She shrank away as I got up close.

"This may be hard for you to understand," I said. "But I'm not a patient. Somebody gave me a shot. How did I get here?"

The woman shook her head. She still looked dubious.

"Someone rang Hire-A-Nurse," she said. "They arranged a flight for you this morning. You are due at a clinic in San Francisco for rest and observation."

I went back over to the cot and stared out the window.

"What name?" I said.

"Faraday," the nurse said.

"That's about the only true statement you were given," I said.

I spotted my clothes about then. They were lying in a neat pile on a wooden seat at the end of the cot. All the cogs of my brain were working now.

"We've got to turn back this aircraft," I said.

The woman's eyes opened wide.

"I'm not crazy," I told her.

She squeaked as I started climbing into my clothes.

"You're a nurse, aren't you?" I said.

I went through my pockets; everything appeared to be intact. Even the Smith-Wesson and webbing holster was bundled inside my jacket. I broke open the gun. All the shells had been removed. The nurse's eyes were like soup-plates in her face when she spotted the gun.

"I'm a private detective," I said. "I've got to get the pilot to turn back."

The woman shrank away as I went over toward the door in the bulkhead. The plane banked again and I stumbled. I fought the mist that threatened to black me out for almost a minute. Then I got my hand on the door-latch and levered myself through. I was fully dressed by this time and I held the empty gun in my inside jacket pocket. I hoped there wouldn't

He had a worried look in his eyes but I had a notion he was beginning to get the point.

"She said you had a gun."

"Sure I've got a gun," I said.

I showed him the Smith-Wesson.

"If I'd been a hi-jacker I'd have used it straight off."

The co-pilot licked his lips. He thought for a moment or two. I could almost see the processes etching themselves across his forehead. The hostess was hovering nervously halfway between him and the far door. He swallowed and then put down the fire-extinguisher on an empty seat behind him.

"What's your suggestion?" he said.

"Get the pilot to turn back to L.A. International." I said. "It could save sixty-five lives."

I looked over his shoulder to where a small dark-haired child had tottered out into the aisle. The co-pilot was still hesitating.

"What if you're wrong?" he said.

253

I shrugged.

"We've still got sixty-five lives intact," I said. "You've lost half an hour of flight-time and I could be arrested for public nuisance."

I held the Smith-Wesson up in front of his face and broke it open.

"It's empty anyway," I said.

The co-pilot grinned.

"I'll buy it," he said. "What are we looking for?"

"Could be in a child's plastic toy," I said.

I followed the co-pilot back down the aisle. He spoke urgently to the hostess and she went into the cabin. I heard the door lock behind her.

"We'd better not make any announcement," I told the co-pilot. "We don't want to start a panic."

He nodded. "I'll go search the luggage compartment."

"You'll find a frightened nurse in there," I said. "She thinks I'm crazy."

The co-pilot grinned again.

"She's not the only one," he said.

The aircraft started turning as he went back toward the rear. There was land beneath the big machine now. I don't think any of the passengers had even noticed. Most of them were dozing in the strong sunshine that filtered through the tinted windows. I went back down the aisle. I looked at my watch. Already another five minutes had gone by. My eyes raked the luggage racks.

If Mayer was acting true to form the bomb should be in one of Troon's plastic toys. I figured I hadn't been sent on this trip for my health. Whoever was blowing up commercial airliners couldn't afford to let me live. I was getting too close to the truth. Whatever that was. Some of the pieces were to hand but I still wanted the major portions. I went back down the aisle once more. The big co-pilot came out the luggage compartment door, the nurse behind him. He spread his hands wide in frustration.

He went unobtrusively down the

left-hand side of the aisle, his hand trailing over the luggage racks. The little dark girl had turned now. She stood in the middle of the aisle sucking her thumb. She held something in the crook of her right arm. Something that I remembered. She smiled at me as I went toward her. I stooped down three yards away and smiled back.

"Let's see him walk, honey," I said.

The little girl crowed with pleasure. She bent and put the furry toy down with pride. I heard a clicking noise. The penguin walked solemnly toward me, the sunlight shining off the glazing of its face, the mouth grinning humorlessly. I caught the toy and picked it up. I could hear a faint ticking inside. Somebody shouted as I started running toward the rear. I could hear the little girl wailing as I brushed past.

The co-pilot had already caught my signal, was slamming at the barred emergency exit with heavy shoulders. I put the penguin down on the seat nearby. Steel claws were scratching across my stomach. I could see the hostess's mouth, a round black O in her face and several of the passengers had got to their feet. The hostess went to soothe them. An argument began farther down the aisle. I joined the co-pilot and we levered the red-painted metal bar upright.

"There'll be a hell of a slip," the co-pilot warned. "For Christ's sake don't get sucked out."

I nodded. I clung with my left hand to the back of the seat as we levered together. The plane had settled up on course and we were over the sea now, about five thousand feet below. The bar gave and the door came outwards with a sucking roar. Wind flapped and screamed at us. I could suddenly see the waves, every foaming ripple clear-cut like a steel engraving.

The door went back on steel hinges and we levered it aside. I got to the penguin as the co-pilot hung on to the door bar. The sound of the engines and the buffeting of the wind seemed to black everything out of my mind. I stood back and threw the mechanical toy as hard and fast as I could through the oblong space in the plane body. It whirled back in the slipstream but it was clear and I could see it falling, a small black oblong against the greeny-white of the sea.

A yellow flash seared the windows of the aircraft; a fraction later a hollow roar reached us and something sucked and buffeted at the big airliner. The door slid back, the co-pilot hanging helplessly on to the bar. The cabin was tilting and passengers were screaming; people were falling in a tangle of arms and legs. I saw one of the windows opposite me suddenly star as though someone had drawn a line along it with a diamond-cutter. I went catapulting backwards over the seats.

It seemed very quiet when I came around. A woman was crying to herself farther down the passenger saloon but there was no panic. The aircraft was flying level and straight. I struggled up and looked out the window. We'd be into L.A. International within a couple of minutes. There seemed a lot of people already streaming on to the tarmac.

The co-pilot helped me up. There was blood on his knuckles and a white, strained look on his face. I saw he'd bolted the emergency door again. The hostess stumbled up toward us.

"Christ, that was close," the co-pilot said.

I nodded. I slumped down into the nearest seat and sat motionless as the aircraft came in. As soon as the wheels touched down I couldn't stop trembling.

19

THERE was an expression on
Tom Dacey's face I hadn't seen
before.

"You've done enough, Mike," he
said. "Best let the official police take
over."

"We haven't got time," I said.
"There's just a few hours to crack this
quickly. Otherwise it will be too late."

I lit my second cigarette and noticed
my fingers were steadier. Stella smiled
at me across the desk.

"You'll note there weren't any Arabs
on this flight," I said.

Dacey nodded. He slumped in the
armchair across from me. I guessed
his neck was on the chopping block
too. I'd got out the Airport in the
confusion without being stopped. I'd
phoned Stella. The airline crew knew
my identity which meant the police

would soon want answers to a lot of questions. Answers I hadn't yet got. So we were using Dacey's office temporarily.

Deirdre Dacey sat opposite. She and Stella hadn't stopped taking notes since we'd come in. Stella smoothed her scratchpad and picked up her coffee cup. She smiled conspiratorially at the other girl.

"The next move?" she said.

I glanced over at Tom Dacey. His usually phlegmatic face looked shattered. These sort of operations were a bit way out for him.

"I've got an indea," I said. "A package deal for the police, wrapping the whole thing up and getting us all off the hook."

Dacey stirred in his seat.

"That sounds more like it," he said. "What do you want us to do?"

"Just tail me when I leave here," I said. "Move in when I signal, not before. Understood?"

Dacey grinned.

261

"You mean we got a choice?"

"It's either that or going up the river," I said.

Dacey rubbed his chin with his big hand.

"We'll play along," he said. "But I'll want to know a little more."

"Fill you in on the way," I said. "It all revolves around a woman's perfume."

I avoided the look in Dacey's eye. His daughter smiled at me.

"It's all right, Mr Dacey," Stella said. "We always operate like this."

Dacey gave her a long look.

"Guess I'll stick to the insurance business," he muttered.

"You got the spare shells?" I said.

Stella pushed the box of slugs over to me and I reloaded the Smith-Wesson.

"You found Reynolds all right?" I said.

Dacey stood up abruptly.

"And the character in the freezer," he said. "The police asked me so many questions I've got enough left over for the next case."

I grinned.

"We'll sort it all out for them in due time."

"Providing they don't catch up with us first," Dacey said.

Stella smiled too.

"They never quite do that, Mr Dacey," she said.

"We'd better go out separately," I said. "If I'm going to be picked up I don't want to involve you."

Deirdre Dacey glanced up from her scratchpad and gave me a warm look. It started raising heat pimples on my skin. I got up and went over toward the door.

"All right, Mike," Dacey said. "We'll be right behind you."

"Not too far," I said.

I went down to the street, picked up the Buick and slid behind the wheel. When I was sure Deirdre Dacey's sport-job was squarely in the rear-mirror, I started making time across town.

It had started raining again when I reached the Bixby Apartments. I walked across the vestibule with the white leather divans and rode up to the fourth floor. Dacey and the girls got in the elevator before it took off but they didn't speak. I got off at the fourth floor leaving them to go on up to the fifth and find their way down again.

I went along the corridor to the fourth door on the right for the second time in my life, the Smith-Wesson making a steady pressure in its harness against my chest muscles and with a big question-mark hanging in the air. I thumbed the satin-steel bellpush of Apartment 42 and waited. The door opened almost immediately and the big, dark-haired man with the black mustache stood framed in the opening.

His eyes went wide with recognition. He was just opening his mouth to say something when I hit him between the eyes. He went crashing back across the entrance and rolled down the staircase that led to the living area. I latched back the door, closed it and ran down after him. He was already groaning and sitting up. I had the Smith-Wesson steady on him as he started to move.

"Just take it nice and slow," I said.

Conrad Weinstock wiped his big hand across his lips. His fingers came away scarlet. There were ugly patches of white around his eyes and mouth.

"Just what the hell does this mean, Faraday?" he said thickly.

"It just means I'm not taking any more chances on this case," I said. "You and Mayer figured me for a one-way ride last night."

Weinstock snorted. He put one hand out to the balustrade and started to drag himself up.

"You mind if I sit down?"

"Get over on the divan," I said. "If anyone disturbs us I start letting holes into your digestive system."

265

Weinstock got up, hanging heavily on to the railing. He looked round the apartment uneasily, like someone might be listening. I saw now he had a raincoat folded at one end of the divan. There were three big pigskin suitcases resting on the floor near the occasional table. A tan briefcase and a couple of magazines were lying near the raincoat.

"Going somewhere?" I said.

I moved in behind Weinstock and he sat down warily in the centre of the big settee. He crossed his legs and scowled at me. I went to stand behind him where I could watch both him and the entire room.

"Just taking a little vacation," he said.

"I'll bet," I told him.

I put the Smith-Wesson barrel on the back of Weinstock's neck. He wriggled uneasily like the barrel was hot.

"I want to know more about the lady whose perfume I smelt here the other afternoon," I said. "I want to know

266

why you stood behind the door and stuck a hypodermic in me yesterday. It was you, wasn't it?"

Weinstock nodded. His body had sagged.

"I was sorry about that," he said. "I didn't know it was you. They said someone was trying to shake them down for blackmail."

I stared at the back of Weinstock's head.

"They only tried to blow me and a planeload of innocent passengers to glory," I said. "You'd better come up with something better than that."

Weinstock turned around to face me. He ignored the pistol barrel. His face looked green in the dim light of the apartment. The rain was tapping at the windows with ghostly fingers.

"You're joking?" he said.

I shook my head.

"You'd better start talking," I said. "You'll be going down for a long time in any case."

Weinstock let out his breath in a

long, expressive hiss.

"Jesus Christ," he said.

He turned back and leaned against the divan. I went around in front and sat on an arm where I could keep an eye on him. Something about him and this set-up didn't fit.

"Mind if I smoke?" Weinstock said.

I passed him my pack. He took an enamelled lighter off the table and lit up before handing the package back to me. I joined him and put my spent match down in a crystal bowl on the table. Weinstock closed his eyes and feathered out smoke through his nostrils.

"I met Carol Twining about a year ago," he said. "She's pretty nice. She and her brother Jack have been good to me. They loaned me money to help me get my factory started. Carol and I are to be married."

He opened his eyes and frowned.

"Trouble is, I can't get a divorce. I've tried all ways but my wife has been raising hell. When you came around the other day I became suspicious when you started spinning me a yarn about plastic toys. Carol said you'd been put on to us by my wife and were bound to make trouble."

I lowered the Smith-Wesson and stared at Weinstock. I'm a pretty good judge of human nature. I was beginning to believe his story.

"Then Jack came to me and said you were trying to put the screws on Carol," Weinstock said. "Blackmail."

I stared.

"Someone's been putting you on," I said. "I don't even know the woman."

Weinstock closed his eyes again like my punch had addled his brains.

"I don't know what the hell to think, Mr Faraday," he said. "I believed it, anyway. Jack said you were coming up here for a shakedown. He said he'd help me get rid of you. If I'd pump you full of dope he'd arrange it so you'd never trouble us again."

"He did," I said grimly.

Weinstock stared at me angrily.

269

"I don't know anything about aircraft," he said. "Jack was going to dump you somewhere in your heap, soak your clothes in booze and get you sent up for drunk driving."

His voice had an unmistakable ring of conviction. I lowered the Smith-Wesson barrel to the floor and sat staring at my toecaps. It was very quiet in the apartment except for the sudden gusting of wind outside.

"You've been taken for the oldest ride in the book," I said. "Your girl friend and her brother had me put aboard a San Francisco flight. If I hadn't tossed the bomb out the door sixty-five people would have died."

Weinstock's lips started to tremble as he stared at me.

"The bomb was packed in a mechanical penguin made by Troon's factory," I said. "The toys were being shipped by Reynolds, an overseer at the plant, and packed with mechanism and explosives by a man who owned La Boutique Fantasque. A man called

Kinross who got himself killed when his usefulness had expired. Like Curtis, one of Troon's truck drivers, who delivered the stuff."

Weinstock's face had gone grey by now. He flinched back on the divan like he was in pain.

"Honest to God, I don't know what you're talking about, Mr Faraday," he said.

"They're the same people who brought down the airliner the other night," I said.

"What made you come here?" Weinstock said.

"A perfume," I told him. "A very distinctive one. I smelt it when you were having the row with your girl-friend the other afternoon. It was the same perfume worn by someone who was watching me at Kinross's shop."

Weinstock nodded.

"It is unusual," he said. "And expensive. It's called Caress."

"Mayer, Kinross's manager acted highly suspicious," I said. "My guess is he's in on it too."

Weinstock shook his head.

"Never heard of him."

"What we want now is Miss Twining and her brother," I said. "You were packing, presumably to meet one or the other of them. I want the meeting place. If your story's true it might help get you off the hook."

Weinstock shook his head.

"Carol and I are to be married," he said.

"Grow up," I told him. "Carol's been blowing up aeroplanes. Besides, you're married already."

I was getting tired of the conversation. The air was still and stuffy in here and perhaps I was getting careless.

"Why would Carol want to do that?" Weinstock said. He looked sick.

"Lots of reasons," I told him. "We'll know when we catch up with her."

Weinstock got up abruptly from the divan. I got up too. The door leading to the bedroom slammed back on its hinges as a big body came through.

The crack of the explosion seemed to lift my head off. The slug smashed glass in rear of us as Weinstock went diving to the ground.

I had the Smith-Wesson up and was pumping shots at the figure of the big man. Splinters of wood flew as he ducked toward the staircase. Mayer had an insane look on his face as he lifted the cannon again. I lifted the Smith-Wesson and got a third off.

Mayer crumpled in mid-stride. His face changed suddenly like a light-bulb going out. The cannon skidded from his hand and went bouncing down the staircase.

Mayer folded in the middle like his body was hinged. I could see blood now on the side of his coat, dripping downwards toward the floor. He went over the ornamental iron railing and crashed flat on to a ceramic-topped table, demolishing it. The silence that crowded in was broken by running feet in the corridor.

Weinstock crawled up to stand next

to me. He looked old and ill.

"Christ," he said.

I went over to look at Mayer.

"You can say that again," I told him.

20

TOM DACEY'S face looked so worried I figured he might burst into tears. He sucked his lower lip and looked at me sombrely as I knelt over Mayer's body. The big man was twitching and moaning noises were coming out his mouth.

"He'll live," I said.

Stella's head had appeared over Dacey's shoulder and I could see Deirdre behind her. Weinstock was kneeling by me. He'd opened Mayer's collar and was trying to staunch the blood in his side with a handkerchief.

"He was lucky," I said. "The bullet went clear through. I guess it was shock more than anything."

"How the hell are we going to explain all this?" Dacey said.

"We'll think of something," I told him.

"Why the hell would he want to do this?" Weinstock said to me.

"I could think of a thousand reasons," I said. "Mayer gave himself away at the Boutique."

Weinstock looked at me like I was crazy.

"I don't know any Mayer," he said. "This is Jack Twining, Carol's brother."

I knelt and stared at him. Cogs were going in my head. I could see Dacey's jaw half-open.

"We got the pieces," I told Weinstock. "If your story's true you got an out."

I leaned past Weinstock and went through the big man's pockets. His eyes were flickering now but he wasn't fully around.

I found some photographs in his wallet and a bundle of letters. There was some money and a lot of other stuff but it was the more personal material that interested me. I took it back over to the divan to sift through it.

"I'll phone the ambulance," Dacey said.

He went over to the phone on the table and dialled. He looked out of his element here. The photographs showed Twining with a striking-looking blonde. They were on a beach together and the way they were acting it didn't look like they were brother and sister. I picked up one of the letters. It was addressed to Mr and Mrs J. Twining. I went through the letters quickly. Weinstock was back over by me now. The two girls were fixing Twining's wound.

"Find anything?" Weinstock said.

"Enough," I told him. "You've been taken for a ride. This character here and Carol Twining were married."

I shoved the letters and pictures into his hand and went over to where Dacey was spitting instructions into the phone mouthpiece. I kept an eye on Weinstock. He had slumped down on the divan and was going through the stuff I'd given him like he couldn't believe what he was reading.

I went back over toward him, avoiding his eyes. He looked like someone for whom the world had just ended. He passed the pictures and documents back with a trembling hand.

"You didn't know Twining was in there?" I said, looking across to where Stella was helping the big man up on to an armchair. Dacey hurried back to give her a hand. Weinstock shook his head.

"Honest to God, Mr Faraday," he said. "Jack was going to meet us at the plane."

"You still got time to clear yourself," I said. "If Twining was going to catch it after he left here it can't have gone."

Weinstock glanced at his watch. The strength had come back into his face as he looked up at me.

"I want some explanations myself. We'll go down to L.A. International, Mr Faraday."

★ ★ ★

It was still raining. Dacey's face was harsh and tired as he spun the wheel of the car and bored in behind a gasoline truck whose driver was hesitating which turn to take. I sat in rear between Stella and Deirdre Dacey and tried to paste my thoughts together. They still weren't making much sense but a more coherent pattern was beginning to emerge. Weinstock sat in front next to Dacey and glanced at his wrist-watch from time to time.

"We got an hour yet," he said for the second time. "The plane doesn't leave until nine."

It was dark now and neons were making mauve and gold stripes along Dacey's face as he turned in toward L.A. International. I hadn't eaten anything today except a couple of sandwiches at Dacey's office and I was beginning to feel hungry. Stella was on my right. She smiled at me affectionately and I felt the soft pressure of her hand in mine at around the same time Deirdre Dacey reached for my left hand. It felt pretty good with the two of them like that and I hoped I wouldn't blow a fuse before we got to the Airport.

"What the hell did you intend to do in Mex. City?" I asked Weinstock.

He craned his head round and appeared surprised at the question.

"We would have worked something out," he said. "Firstly, Carol and I wanted to be alone together. I hoped my wife might divorce me once she knew we were there."

"What was Jack Twining going to do?" I said. "Act as chaperone?"

Weinstock scowled.

"If he lives I'll ask him," he said in a nasty voice.

"He'll live," I said. "The intern said it looked like the slug had missed anything vital."

The car lurched as Dacey swung the wheel and I could see the Airport buildings coming up through the rainshimmer and the dusk. Dacey spun the wheel again and turned off the approach tunnel and drew up before a steel-mesh gate which had a big white on red board with: AUTHORISED PERSONNEL ONLY. He got out and spoke with the uniformed guard in rear of the gate. I guessed he was well known around the Airport because he didn't have to show any authority. The guard nodded and opened up the gate.

Dacey came back and slid behind the wheel with a grunt. He eased the automobile through the opening. I could see a second guard phoning through the windows of a small hut. The first guard, a tall, lean man with swarthy features flicked his eyes over us.

"You'd best go straight to Lieutenant Allcock of Airport Security," he said laconically. "We've warned him you're on your way over."

Dacey nodded. He put the car in gear. The drizzle was blurring the windscreen again and he started the wipers. The silvery shapes of parked aircraft slid by in the dusk. Dacey was using a non-public road and he evidently knew where to go. We drove about two miles between hangars and administration buildings. Somewhere near the main reception buildings Dacey pulled up in a loading bay and we got out.

The rain was sheeting down now and we sprinted for shelter. Dacey led the way down a concrete tunnel which was loud with speaker announcements. We got out on a tiled concourse.

"What's your flight?" Dacey said.

"No. 304. Gate 12," Weinstock told him.

He glanced at his watch. There was just fifty minutes to go.

"You figure she'll be there?" I said as we pounded across the concourse.

"She'll be there," Weinstock said. "She'll be expecting Twining, won't she?"

There were bitter undertones to his voice. I didn't blame him. I knew how

I'd have felt in his position. I fell in between Stella and Deirdre Dacey. This was Dacey's show and I'd let him handle it from now on in. Unless there was any rough stuff, of course. Three large men in dark suits were waiting in front of the discreetly situated Airport Police Office. The tallest and squarest of them gave Dacey a chunky hand to shake. Brief introductions were made. Lieutenant Allcock gave me a flash of his square teeth. He looked like Khruschev on his afternoon off.

"We want authority to run over Flight 304 without any fuss." Dacey said.

Allcock looked over our group wryly.

"All of you?" he said dubiously.

"The girls can stay at the boarding gate," Dacey said. "It'll act as an extra check. Besides, we don't want to expose them to unnecessary danger."

Allcock's interest quickened.

"Like that, is it?" he said.

He led the way in rear of the office to a tarmac area where several Airport

Police cars were parked. The other two men got in one car and the six of us into the automobile driven by Allcock. We followed the first car, Allcock driving fast and quietly, without using any sirens or flashing lights. I liked that bit. The other car had already stopped in a restricted parking bay near Gate 12 and the other two officers were waiting for us as we piled out.

"We're looking for a girl called Carol Twining," Dacey said. "She's supposed to be meeting Mr Weinstock here."

Allcock grunted and led the way up the concourse to where passengers were milling around the entrance to Gate 12. Allcock ignored the queue and went up toward the gate officials, leaving us in rear. I didn't want to tip our hand in case the girl showed. She might be already in the queue come to that. Weinstock was grim and taciturn. I could guess what thoughts were tumbling around in his head. His face looked old and shrunken.

Stella wore a white slicker and sou-wester and the rain shone in sparkling droplets on the bright bell of her hair. I could see Deirdre Dacey quietly assessing her. It would have been amusing any other time but right now it was out of place. Dacey stood apart from the group and kept his eye fixed on the gate.

"Let us know if you see her," he said suddenly to Weinstock.

"Don't worry," the big man said. "You'll be the first to know."

Allcock was away about five minutes. I could see him bending over a flight-list on a clipboard being held by a slim air-hostess. Beyond the glass windows that led to the apron the gleaming hull of a Boeing 707 glistened under the lights and the rain. The big Lieutenant came back at last. He shook his head at Dacey's interrogative look.

"Nobody named Twining on the flight schedule," he said.

Weinstock looked incredulous. He cleared his throat with an effort.

"There must be some mistake," he said.

The Airport man looked at him carefully.

"No mistake, Mr Weinstock," he said. "You're down all right. Apparently the Twinings cancelled out."

Dacey turned to me. His face looked set and heavy.

"Looks like we're wasting our time here," he said.

I shook my head.

"Not necessarily. This doesn't fit with their track record. Can we get a search of this aircraft?"

Allcock nodded.

"Nothing easier."

He lifted his hand and the two officers in dark clothes materialized at his elbow. He gave them instructions in clipped tones. They went away in the direction of the aircraft.

"I'd like a look at the passengers," I said. "The girls can stay here."

Allcock led the way toward Gate 12. Weinstock and I followed with Dacey bringing up the rear. The passengers were just starting to go through. I turned up my collar as we got out on to the tarmac. The rain was cold now and there was a slight wind gusting at the Airport buildings. The scream of a jet came downwind, muffled by the surrounding structures, then suddenly sharp and savage as it left the apron and got into the open.

Allcock was sprinting and I left the others and joined him. We got to the foot of the gangway about a hundred feet ahead of the first passengers. The hostess, a dark-haired girl with a nice build was just coming down the steps. I could see one of the plain-clothes men looking out the cabin window toward us. Allcock and I walked back down, looking the passengers over casually as they came up. Weinstock and Dacey had joined us now.

I didn't see anything unusual. There was a group of about a dozen nuns, chattering excitedly like school-children; a mixture of businessmen; some young couples; a few children; two elderly parsons in dog-collars. I could see the rage and bafflement in Weinstock's eyes. He fell in beside me as I went back toward the aircraft steps.

I stopped and stared. I could see the air-hostess through the shimmering droplets of rain. Something in her face seemed vaguely familiar. Two small children were just going aboard. The hostess had stooped, was pushing something into the little boy's hands. It was another of the yellow plastic ducks I was beginning to hate.

I was at the girl's side in two strides, Weinstock behind me. The girl looked at me blankly as I reached the gang-way. Her eyes opened wide in recognition. I scooped up the duck in one hand and pulled the children back. The passengers had stopped in astonishment.

"This is one thing Flight 304 won't be needing," I said, holding up the plastic toy.

The hostess ducked back as I reached

for her with my right hand. Her face was a mask of fear and rage. I had her raven-black hair in my hand now. I tugged sharply and the dark wig fell away to reveal the honey-blonde hair of Janet Firestone.

289

21

THE girl's eyes were like those of dead butterflies. The sudden scream as the Boeing engines started up set my teeth on edge. Weinstock stood like a man turned to stone. The group of passengers halted at the gangway seemed like figures frozen in a photograph. I must have been a bit off balance too. Before I had time to react the girl tore the plastic duck out of my hands. Her movement was like a whiplash. She adjusted something at the rear of the toy.

"Try anything and we all get blown to pieces," she said.

She stepped backwards, moving delicately, away from the aircraft.

"The jig's up," I said. "Your husband's in hospital. You've got no cards any more."

The white set mask of the girl's face

cracked momentarily and her mouth trembled. The jet engine revved up so that she had to shout to make herself heard.

"There's always a way, Mr Faraday," she said.

Something about the set of her figure and the way she was holding the plastic duck communicated itself to the passengers. They started backing away. I gestured to them.

"Best do as the lady says," I told them. "She has a bomb."

Out the corner of my eye I could see Dacey and the big figure of Allcock coming up in rear of the queue. Weinstock hadn't said anything yet but now his breath rasped in my ear.

"I was going to take the trip alone," he said. "A one-way ticket with an explosion at the end of it."

Janet Firestone smiled a hard, tight-mouthed smile.

"That's the way it goes sometimes, lover," she said.

She was about five yards from

us now, walking slowly backwards, watching us and the passengers. Some of the nuns were on their knees and I could see a woman with two children pressing them down on to the tarmac of the apron. Dacey and the big Lieutenant had swivelled to face the girl but otherwise they weren't making any moves. The engines suddenly throttled back and I found I could make my voice heard.

"The lady has a bomb," I repeated for Allcock's benefit.

The crowd wavered and started to melt back toward the Airport buildings. Weinstock took two paces toward the girl and stopped.

"There's nowhere to go," I told her.

"I'll be the best judge of that," Janet Firestone said. "Just stay where you are."

I put out my hand and caught Weinstock's arm.

"It's not worth getting killed at this stage," I told him. "Let the regular boys handle it."

I could already see Lieutenant Allcock on his way back to the loading gate. Someone must have radioed the pilot from the tower because the big Boeing jet's engines suddenly cut out. An unnatural silence crowded in. The girl was ten yards off now, her blue-uniformed figure beginning to merge with the shadows.

Now I could see only the pale oval of her face. I had the Smith-Wesson out, though I couldn't figure what good it would do. Force of habit I guess.

"That damn hard-faced bitch," Weinstock gritted.

He turned a face to me that looked like hammered sheet-iron.

"We're not letting her get away with this."

I shrugged.

"I don't see the alternative. I've no objection to the lady going skyward but we've got the passengers and Airport staff to consider."

Weinstock's hard, flinty face seemed to crumple.

"Guess you're right," he said.

Then he'd turned and was running in a zig-zag pattern around the tail of the Boeing. I swore. I was a little slow off the mark tonight. There was no sign of the girl in the gloom when I got round the tail myself, but I could see Weinstock about a hundred yards ahead. I put on a spurt and got to within a yard of him.

"You're crazy," I said.

Weinstock didn't stop but he turned his head.

"She's heading for the loading tunnel," he said. "We got a chance there."

I saw what he meant. A dim oblong glow was eating up the darkness ahead. Stencilled against it was the very small, black figure of the girl, running with long strides like an athlete. We were in among crates and fork-lift trucks by now. A burly character in overalls shouted as we pounded by. His words were chopped into segments by another jet motor which started up out on the apron.

Weinstock had gained a little when I swerved but I could see him against the light from the tunnel. He must have been in pretty hard condition for a man of his age.

He was still going pretty fast but I was gaining on him now. The tunnel entrance was climbing up the sky and it cast a glow across the aisles between the crates and boxes which the personnel were stacking with fork-lift trucks ready for loading. I could see the far-off figure of the girl, disappearing down the slope which led to the tunnel. Weinstock, still going hard, skidded on the wet tarmac and almost went down so that I was nearly up with him by the time we reached the far slope.

The rain was coming down pretty heavily and I spotted some pools of oil on the ground in the light coming up from the tunnel entrance so I slowed down. Beyond, the area was drier and then I was in the mouth of the white-tiled entrance. Light came from heavy-duty tubes in heavy mountings bolted to the walls of the tunnel. It was empty except for the figure of the girl about three hundred yards ahead. She was going incredibly fast. Like I said, she must have been an athlete.

Weinstock had stopped as I covered the last hundred yards down toward him. He was crouched, supporting himself with one arm against the tunnel wall, squinting along the barrel of the chrome-plated pistol he'd produced from somewhere. I put on a spurt but it was too late. The shot slapped out and went re-echoing along the walls of the tunnel. The figure of the girl jumped like a doll on a string.

Something sucked and licked at us along the tunnel and flame grew until it was of eye-aching intensity. I saw Weinstock's body twisted against the glare, his hands over his eyes. Then the tunnel wall came up to meet me and I was swept helplessly along by a great wind which beat over us and a deafening noise roared in the ears and drowned everything else.

When I came around there was choking dust in my mouth and pieces of debris still pattering around so I couldn't have been out more than a second or two. There was a weight across my legs. I struggled up and got Weinstock upright. His eyes were wide and unseeing.

"I aimed wide," he said in a hushed voice.

"Don't blame yourself," I said. "It probably blew up of itself. Those gadgets can never be made really reliable."

The thin noise of sirens came across the Airport tarmac and with it the beat of running feet. A great cloud of acrid smoke blocked the tunnel ahead. There was the smell of death in it.

I went down with a handkerchief pressed over my mouth. There was nothing there but a great gaping hole in the concrete floor of the tunnel. Tiles had been stripped from the walls for hundreds of yards in each direction and most of the lights were out. There

was just enough for me to see the few
scraps of cloth which represented all
that was left of Janet Firestone. It
was poetic justice. I was still thinking
about it when Dacey and the others
came up.

★ ★ ★

Stella came back and put the cup of
coffee down on the blotter in front
of me.

"Don't forget you're due down at
Police H.Q. in an hour," she said.

"As if I could forget," I told her.

I sipped the coffee and sat at my
broadtop looking at the stalled traffic
on the boulevard below. It was raining
again and the moisture on the sidewalks
made a pallid sheen through the exhaust
fumes.

"Troon rang in," Stella said. "He
and Myriam Van Cleef are coming over
this afternoon. He said he wouldn't
forget what you'd done for him and
his business."

"As long as he doesn't forget my bill," I said. "Besides, I haven't done anything for him."

Stella grinned across at me. She looked particularly desirable this morning. But then she always does.

"He seems to think you have," she said. "There's some talk of him and Miss Van Cleef getting engaged."

"Bully for her," I said.

Stella frowned.

"Haven't you got it the wrong way round?"

"I don't think so," I told her. "She was making all the running."

Stella consulted her scratchpad again.

"Dacey was on too. He said he'd see you at Police H.Q. His daughter wants you to go over for dinner tonight."

"That's great," I said. "They may let me out on parole."

Stella smiled again.

"What was the whole thing about, Mike? Just for the record."

"Plain simple insurance," I said. "Twining talked. He ought to draw

299

thirty years if they're lenient. He and the girl worked it out between them."

Stella wrinkled up her brows.

"Was she Janet Firestone or not?"

"Until recently," I said. "She and Twining were married all right. The Firestone number had a rich uncle. She insured him for a million dollars and then blew the plane up. With the help of the character at La Boutique Fantasque, of course."

Stella made a face as she sipped her coffee.

"Nice people," she said.

"That isn't all of it," I said. "Twining had a rich relative too. An aunt. She was on the plane which blew up at Montreal two months ago."

There was a heavy silence in the office as Stella looked at me incredulously.

"The aunt was insured for a million also," I said. "These were big operators. They wanted the authorities to think there were Arab terrorists involved, so they chose flights which had Arab passengers."

"It would take them a hell of a time to collect," Stella said dubiously.

"They could afford to wait," I said. "What about the message sent to the Firestone girl's uncle?" Stella said.

I shook my head.

"They cooked that up after his plane had left."

Stella got up and came over to my desk. She sat down on the edge of it, holding her coffee cup in one hand and swinging a long, shapely leg.

"Why would she want to come and consult you, Mike?"

"This girl had all the nerve in the world," I said. "As soon as Troon called me in, she wanted to know the state of the game. They were planning to get rid of the old man. She didn't know what I might turn up. So she came to consult me."

"So she could keep an eye on things," Stella said slowly. "Cool stuff."

"That's not all," I said. "She was a nympho too. She had Weinstock going a long time ago. His connection with the plastic toy industry set her mind working on the bomb idea. He changed his factory and set-up just about the time she was ready to move so she made contact with Reynolds. Weinstock would have been a prime suspect if anything had gone wrong."

I got up and went to look out the window. Stella's legs were beginning to distract my attention.

"When I turned up at the Apartments she figured I was getting too close," I said. "Janet Firestone couldn't be connected with Carol Twining. She was with Weinstock in the crowd going into the bar but I didn't spot him. But I saw his back when he was phoning the apartment to warn Twining I was on my way up."

Stella had come up behind me now. I could see her golden hair reflected in the rain-streaked glass of the window.

"Weinstock thinking you were black-mailing the girl," she said.

"That's about it. Then Weinstock lit out for the apartment ahead of me just in time to jab me with the hypodermic when I showed up."

"His last useful job," Stella said. "He would have ended up in little pieces if you hadn't remembered the girl's perfume."

"Not to mention a hundred other passengers," I said.

"What do you think will happen to him?" Stella said.

"Over Janet Firestone?" I said. "They ought to give him a medal. Besides, I don't think he had anything to do with the girl's death. The thing just went off, perhaps because of the heat of her hand."

Stella was silent for a long minute. Then she came closer to me and put her head up against my cheek.

"You'd better be getting on downtown," she said. "You've a lot of explaining to do."

"I don't think I've forgotten anything," I said.

"If you have the police will remember for you," Stella said.

I stood finishing my cigarette, looking down at the stalled traffic on the boulevard; not seeing the traffic or hearing the rain but thinking instead of a girl with a face like an angel who had killed over two hundred people in order to make sure of two.

Stella put up a warm hand and fondled my ear.

"If that perfume was so distinctive, Mike, why didn't you spot it when the Firestone girl first came to the office?"

"I did," I said. "But I didn't put it together until later. I had plenty other things to think about."

"Like today's hearing," Stella said. She brushed a piece of lint from my collar and bent forward to kiss my cheek. I felt it all the way down to my fallen arches.

"You never do quite lose your licence," she said. "See you tomorrow."

"Tonight," I said. "I promised to take you over to dinner at the Daceys."

I left Stella there and rode down in

304

the elevator to the street. I went and picked up the Buick and fought my way through the smog and the rain and the stalled traffic, not thinking about them or the coming interview but instead just Stella's face as I went out the door. By the time I reached Police H.Q. I was almost smiling.

THE END

PRINT-OUT
NIGHT FROST
THE LONELY PLACE
CRACK IN THE SIDEWALK

Other titles in the
Linford Mystery Library:

A GENTEEL LITTLE MURDER
Philip Daniels

Gilbert had a long-cherished plan to murder his wife. When the polished Edward entered the scene Gilbert's attitude was suddenly changed.

DEATH AT THE WEDDING
Madelaine Duke

Dr. Norah North's search for a killer takes her from a wedding to a private hospital.

MURDER FIRST CLASS
Ron Ellis

Will Detective Chief Inspector Glass find the Post Office robbers before the Executioner gets to them?

A FOOT IN THE GRAVE
Bruce Marshall

About to be imprisoned and tortured in Buenos Aires, John Smith escapes, only to become involved in an aeroplane hijacking.

DEAD TROUBLE
Martin Carroll

Trespassing brought Jennifer Denning more than she bargained for. She was totally unprepared for the violence which was to lie in her path.

HOURS TO KILL
Ursula Curtiss

Margaret went to New Mexico to look after her sick sister's rented house and felt a sharp edge of fear when the absent landlady arrived.

THE DEATH OF ABBE DIDIER
Richard Grayson

Inspector Gautier of the Sûreté investigates three crimes which are strangely connected.

NIGHTMARE TIME
Hugh Pentecost

Have the missing major and his wife met with foul play somewhere in the Beaumont Hotel, or is their disappearance a carefully planned step in an act of treason?

BLOOD WILL OUT
Margaret Carr

Why was the manor house so oddly familiar to Elinor Howard? Who would have guessed that a Sunday School outing could lead to murder?

THE DRACULA MURDERS
Philip Daniels

The Horror Ball was interrupted by a spectral figure who warned the merrymakers they were tampering with the unknown.

THE LADIES
OF LAMBTON GREEN
Liza Shepherd

Why did murdered Robin Colquhoun's picture pose such a threat to the ladies of Lambton Green?

CARNABY
AND THE GAOLBREAKERS
Peter N. Walker

Detective Sergeant James Aloysius Carnaby-King is sent to prison as bait. When he joins in an escape he is thrown headfirst into a vicious murder hunt.

MUD IN HIS EYE
Gerald Hammond

The harbourmaster's body is found mangled beneath Major Smyle's yacht. What is the sinister significance of the illicit oysters?

THE SCAVENGERS
Bill Knox

Among the masses of struggling fish in the *Tecta*'s nets was a larger, darker, ominously motionless form . . . the body of a skin diver.

DEATH IN ARCADY
Stella Phillips

Detective Inspector Matthew Furnival works unofficially with the local police when a brutal murder takes place in a caravan camp.

STORM CENTRE
Douglas Clark

Detective Chief Superintendent Masters, temporarily lecturing in a police staff college, finds there's more to the job than a few weeks relaxation in a rural setting.

THE MANUSCRIPT MURDERS
Roy Harley Lewis

Antiquarian bookseller Matthew Coll, acquires a rare 16th century manuscript. But when the Dutch professor who had discovered the journal is murdered, Coll begins to doubt its authenticity.

SHARENDEL
Margaret Carr

Ruth didn't want all that money. And she didn't want Aunt Cass to die. But at Sharendel things looked different. She began to wonder if she had a split personality.

MURDER TO BURN
Laurie Mantell

Sergeants Steven Arrow and Lance Brendon, of the New Zealand police force, come upon a woman's body in the water. When the dead woman is identified they begin to realise that they are investigating a complex fraud.

YOU CAN HELP ME
Maisie Birmingham

Whilst running the Citizens' Advice Bureau, Kate Weatherley is attacked with no apparent motive. Then the body of one of her clients is found in her room.

DAGGERS DRAWN
Margaret Carr

Stacey Manston was the kind of girl who could take most things in her stride, but three murders were something different . . .